THE MAKESHIFT HUSBAND

HILDA STAHL

Published by
Bethel Publishing Company
1819 South Main Street
Elkhart, Indiana 46516

Cover Illustration by Ed French
Edited by Grace Pettifor

Printed in the United States of America

ISBN 0-934998-48-5

In memory of
Mrs. Norman (Hilda) Stahl
who on March 27, 1993
went to be with the Savior
whom she loved and served.

Hilda, you will be greatly missed.
Because of your writing,
the call on your life to help others
will continue.

CHAPTER 1

Labor pains tightened painfully around her and Diane McGraw sank to her knees on the frozen ground with a groan that started deep inside. She could feel the chill on her knees through her blue wool dress and white muslin petticoats. Could she go on? Would 1891 be as cheerless as last year? Maybe it would be better to die on the bleak Nebraska prairie than face another day of a loveless marriage to Seth McGraw.

Diane whimpered. Her gray, wool coat kept out some of the cold January wind. Her warm, gray wool bonnet lined with red satin kept her blonde hair from tangling in the wind. Nothing could keep her heart from feeling dead. Slowly, awkwardly she pushed herself up. "I won't give up no matter how I feel about Seth," she whispered as she pulled her coat over her round stomach. After all, she was Morgan Clements' daughter! Besides, she loved her baby and she would not let him die! She always referred to the baby as *him* even though she knew full well it could be a girl. Girl or boy, she really didn't care. After almost nine months of carrying the baby, she loved him with a fierceness she'd never experienced before.

Glancing up at the snow-threatening sky, Diane trembled.

It looked the same as two weeks ago when a blizzard had roared down from the Dakotas without warning, leaving Seth stranded halfway between home and town. He had managed to make it to Gary Wendall's place and was stuck there for three days. Home by herself, she struggled to keep the fire going and do the chores, continually worrying that Seth had been caught in the open and died. Now another blizzard threatened that might keep her from reaching Pa's ranch or keep Seth from getting there before the baby was born. Diane clenched her fists inside the mittens she'd knitted last fall. "I don't care if you make it, Seth McGraw! I don't care if I ever see you again!"

She gasped and clamped her hand over her mouth. Had she really said that? In the nine months since they were married, she'd never said one word about being unhappy. When she married Seth she was sure she would learn to love him. He was kind and considerate. Before they were married he had acted as if he cared for her, but after the wedding he became withdrawn and quiet. At times he acted as if he was angry at her. She remembered the day she had told him that she was expecting a baby. Instead of rejoicing with her, he stormed out of the house and didn't return for hours. After that, he tried to act pleased and had even helped her decide on names, but all along, she knew he was only pretending to care. The past nine months had been the worst in her life - even worse than when Ma had died. Pa had married Laurel Bennett, the school teacher at Broken Arrow, and brought her home to be their ma. Diane had learned to love Laurel and call her Ma, but she never forgot the agony of her own mother's death. And neither would she forget the agony Seth caused her. She had managed to overlook Seth's coldness and anger most of the time until yesterday.

He'd walked into the kitchen where she was sewing another gown for the baby. The fire in the cast iron cook-stove kept the kitchen cozy and warm.

Scowling, he'd motioned to the gown, "Is that all you ever do?"

Tears filled her eyes. "I thought you'd be happy about the baby." She had been so sure that he was like Pa and wanted a family.

"Did you really think I'd want *this* baby?" he asked coldly.

She had looked at him with a troubled frown. He was very different from what she had expected. She laid down the soft yellow gown and studied him. "Why won't you tell me what's bothering you so much, Seth?"

"Look in your heart and you'll know," he snapped.

She frowned helplessly. "Just tell me!"

"You already know! Stop pretending you don't!" He had rushed back outdoors, clamping his wide-brimmed hat on his bright red hair.

She'd burst into tears and couldn't finish the gown. What had he meant? What was bothering him? She didn't know the answer then and she didn't know it now.

With the wind tugging at her coattails, Diane pushed herself up and pulled the coat tightly around her. In all the years she'd known Seth, she had never seen him act so heartless. "He's sorry he married me," she whispered hoarsely. She gasped, her hand over her heart. Never having admitted it before, she now knew it was true. Glancing over her shoulder toward Seth's ranch hidden behind several hills, she declared, "I'm just as sorry, Seth! Maybe even sorrier!"

Holding her skirts off the frozen ground, she walked on. This afternoon when the pains had persisted she'd left a note for Seth saying she was going to Pa's and to pick her up. She hadn't mentioned the pains because they might be false labor like Ma had said could happen. The baby wasn't due until the end of January and it was only the beginning.

Another pain gripped her and Diane cried out but the cry was lost in the vastness of the prairie. Seth's land butted up to Pa's so there wasn't another place in sight for miles. She sank to her knees again and held herself until the pain subsided. Maybe this was the real thing. Maybe the baby was coming.

Suddenly she heard the loud bellow of a bull. Gasping with fright, she looked over her shoulder to see Seth's new hereford bull charging toward her. Steam rose from its nose and clumps of frozen ground flew out from its hooves. The bull was massive, and with its winter hair, looked even bigger.

Frantically Diane pushed herself up and half-ran, half-walked toward the barbed wire fence that separated Seth's land from Pa's. She had to reach the other side of the fence before the bull attacked her. Fear pricked her skin and shivers ran up and down her spine. She felt the ground shake and was sure she could feel the bull's breath on her neck. Her long skirts hiked up, she ran along the fence until she found sagging wires, then stepped on the bottom two wires and lifted the top two and crawled through, feeling older than her twenty-five years and more awkward than she'd ever felt in her life. The bull was almost on her.

A barb snagged her bonnet and she jerked it free. Just as the bull slid to a stop, she stood up on the other side of the fence, trembling so much she almost fell.

The bull roared and pawed the ground.

"Go back where you belong!" she shouted.

The bull bellowed again, then turned and walked away.

Diane breathed deeply to steady the wild beating of her heart. Pushing strands of blonde hair back, she replaced her bonnet with trembling hands, then pressed her hands to the small of her back and moaned. If the bull would have noticed her sooner, she never would have outrun it. She cried out, then bit her lip. She was safe now.

Abruptly the cold Nebraska wind blew harder and whipped down the valley to her, sending a chill to her bones. She had to keep walking or she would freeze to death. Coyotes would eat her and leave part of her behind like they did with the calves. Maybe her bones would be picked clean before anyone found her. She shivered, then scowled. "Stop it, Diane! You're not a tenderfoot!"

Slowly, carefully, she walked around a hill and through a valley. Up above, the gray sky stretched on and on until it touched the darker gray hills. She felt as if she were the only person alive. The two miles to Pa's ranch seemed more like twenty-two.

Suddenly a man on a big black horse rode into sight. Diane stopped short, her hand to her racing heart. It was Bobby Ryder! Her pulse leaped and she felt weak all over. Would she ever stop loving him even though he was a wild cowboy who drank and smoked and swore and looked at every woman as a conquest? He had no plans for his future except to be a cowboy, ride in local rodeos for fun, and get drunk every Saturday night. But he had charm. He could charm the coldest woman alive and make her love him.

Taking a deep breath, Diane tried to ignore her great desire for Bobby. He hadn't noticed her yet. Maybe he'd ride on without seeing her. She frowned. What was he doing on Pa's land? She shrugged. What did it matter? He was here and so was she. If he didn't see her, she'd call out to him. She couldn't let him ride away without speaking to him, without having him smile his special smile at her.

She'd known him from the time he was eight years-old and she was six and in first grade. Even then he'd charmed her, giving her candy sticks and showing her special places to hide during hide-and-seek at recess.

In sixth grade was when she'd fallen in love with him. She smiled as she remembered how it had happened.

During that year she carried Ma's diary to school with her every day so she would feel like Ma was with her. Ma had had the same blonde hair, blue eyes, and slight build as Diane. Ma had written how she fell in love with Morgan Clements and how she felt when she married him, then how she had felt when they had children. She wrote in great detail about Hadley, Diane, and Worth being born and growing daily. Diane had the places about herself memorized.

The other kids at school teased her about the diary. Even Bobby Ryder had teased her. Seth McGraw hadn't and she liked him because of it.

One day after morning recess she reached in her desk to take out the diary. It was gone! Her heart stood still and she cried in an anguished voice, "Who took my diary?"

Mr. Kurtis looked up from helping Worth with his reading and frowned at her. "Miss Clements, what is the problem?"

"Somebody took my diary!" Tears streamed down her face but she didn't care. She couldn't survive without Ma's diary!

The boys laughed and the girls giggled.

Scowling, Mr. Kurtis rapped his heavy ruler on the desk - the very ruler he used to spank anyone who was unruly. "Students! Mind your manners!" His dark brows met over his large nose as he frowned at everyone. "I want Diane's diary returned to her before school lets out today." He turned back to Worth. "Read page 99 again."

Diane brushed away her tears and tried to work her arithmetic. It was hard to concentrate. She knew Mr. Kurtis would make the person responsible return the diary. But what if he or she dropped the diary down the hole in the toilet?

Seth leaned forward and whispered, "I'm sorry about the diary. I'll make sure you get it back."

She smiled at him and felt better. Secretly she loved Seth even though he was shy and very seldom talked to her. He had beautiful red hair and eyes as blue as hers. He always chose her to be on his side in any games they played at recess. Once he'd stopped Elmer from putting a snake down her back. She whispered, "Thank you, Seth."

"I'd do anything for you, Diane," he said so softly that she wondered if she'd heard right.

At noon recess Diane walked around the schoolyard with her friend Kate Mayberry. Warm wind blew Kate's beautiful, long, black hair across the back of her brown and yellow calico dress. Diane's blonde hair was braided and hung over the shoulder of her blue and red calico dress.

"Whoever took your diary is mean," Kate said.

"I know." It was hard for Diane to talk without bursting into tears again.

"Bobby Ryder is the meanest boy in school. Maybe he took it."

Diane shook her head, "He's never mean to me."

"He is to me!" Kate touched her black hair. "He cut off a big chunk of my hair last week! I hate him!"

Diane gasped, "Kate, you can't hate anybody! Jesus says to love others, even those who do bad things to you."

Just then Bobby Ryder ran around the schoolhouse with his hand behind his back. His hair and eyes were as black as an Indian's and his denim pants were too short. His eyes flashed as he stopped right in front of Diane. "Guess what I have, then you can have it."

Diane's heart leaped, "My diary?"

With a laugh he held it out. His hands were dirty as usual. "I saw Seth McGraw hide it in the woodpile, so I got it out and brought it to you."

Love for Seth died in her heart and love for Bobby sprang full-bloom instead. She gently held the diary to her heart. "Thank you, Bobby!" Right then and there she decided when she grew up she'd marry Bobby Ryder.

Bobby smiled and swaggered away.

Diane had watched him go, then caught sight of Seth at the side of the school. He had a strickened look on his face. She glared at him. He started to speak, then slowly turned and walked away with his red head down and his shoulders bent.

"I hate him," Diane said to Kate. "From now on I'll love only Bobby Ryder."

Diane and Bobby had attended box socials and other functions together. He had called her his girl, but he never spoke of marriage. After he hired on at Nick Stone's ranch and fell in with the other cowboys, he soon became just like them. But her love had remained.

One day last spring, after deliberately staying away

from him all winter, she saw him riding around the lake between Pa's ranch and Nick Stone's. Boldly she rode up to him even though she knew she shouldn't be alone with him.

"Howdy, Bobby." Her cheeks felt on fire, but she wanted to hear his voice and see the twinkle in his dark eyes. She reined in beside him and smiled.

He pulled off his wide-brimmed hat and laughed in delight. "Diane! Is it you or am I seeing an angel?"

She laughed self-consciously. She was glad she was wearing her new pink shirt and Worth's levis. "Are you looking for strays?"

"Sure am." He pulled off his glove and caught her hand. "But I have time to talk to you. I didn't see much of you all winter."

"I know." His touch sent tingles all over her body. "I was teaching school for a while."

"I wish I'd known and I'd have stopped in. Is the desk that I carved *Bobby loves Diane* on still there?"

She flushed and nodded. Many times she'd rubbed her finger over the names and dreamed of marrying Bobby and living happily ever after with him.

He leaped off his horse and lifted her down beside him. His levis fit snugly against his muscled legs. His blue plaid shirt was stained with sweat.

Her heart raced with him so near. He pulled her close and she let him. Her breath caught in her throat. He was going to kiss her. This time she'd let him. He pressed his lips to hers and she felt the kiss down to her toes. She smelled sweat and leather and heard their horses moving restlessly. She returned his kiss with mounting passion. She'd wanted him to kiss her since sixth grade, but hadn't allowed him to, even though he'd begged her. Why had she refused his kisses? They were better in real life than in her daydreams.

"I want you, Di," he whispered gruffly against her ear.

And she wanted him! It embarrassed her to feel her response to him, but she couldn't help herself. What would it matter if she gave herself to him? They loved each other. Just as she was ready to give in to him, she heard a voice inside her saying, "Keep yourself pure for your husband." She groaned and pushed Bobby away. "No!"

"What do you mean 'no'?"

"I can't do what you want! Don't ask me to."

His face darkened with anger. "You're nothing but a tease!"

"I'm sorry." Tears had filled her eyes. "I was wrong to let you kiss me. I won't give myself to anyone but my husband."

He swore at her, then mounted his black horse in one easy movement and rode away.

She leaned weakly against her horse and whispered, "Heavenly Father, thank you for saving me. I'm sorry for putting myself in such a terrible situation."

After a long time she rode home, vowing never again to be alone with Bobby Ryder. She knew she would have to do something to keep from giving in to him. But what? He would find her and at a weak moment, persuade her to give in.

Two days after that, Seth McGraw stopped by to talk to Pa about buying a horse from him. She watched Pa and Seth together. Seth was a few inches taller and leaner than Pa. They were very much alike in nature and they loved and respected each other. Seth was handsome in his levis and blue shirt with the cuffs rolled up on his freckled arms. He was laughing at something Pa had said. Right then and there, she decided she would marry Seth McGraw. In school he'd been shy and hard working, but always nice to her. The only mean thing he ever did was to take her diary, but now it didn't seem all that important. His parents had left him their ranch when they decided to move on to Oregon two years ago, so he had a place of his own with a nice house and barn. Seth was a hard worker with a strong faith in God. He was all Bobby wasn't.

Before Seth left she saw him alone near the corral and hurried to join him. He flushed, making his freckles blend together, but he didn't walk away. She smiled at him as she stood in front of him. "Don't you ever get lonely in that house all by yourself, Seth?"

He smiled and nodded. "Sure do. You got a solution in mind?"

"You could send for a mail-order bride." She watched his eyes carefully for a sign. He looked at her with such intensity that she blushed.

He pulled off his hat and held it between his hands. His red hair was like a flame. He narrowed his blue eyes. "I don't reckon I'd settle for a mail-order bride," he said softly.

Her heart fluttered. "Why is that?"

He shrugged.

She moistened her dry lips as she looked past him at the horses milling in the corral, then back at him. "I bet you never kissed a girl before, have you?"

"Not yet." He leaned against the corral fence and smiled, watching her closely.

Breathlessly, trembling at her own boldness, she stepped close to him. "I dare you to kiss me, Seth McGraw!"

"Do you now?" Laughing softly, he pulled her close and kissed her.

She returned his kiss eagerly.

Seth had smiled and said, "Don't dare me again or I'll kiss you again."

She laughed. "I won't stop you."

He touched her cheek and slowly kissed her again. Not long after that they were married in the church in Broken Arrow and she moved into his two-story frame house. But he had changed from the happy man she knew into a quiet, sometimes angry, man. He only kissed her in the darkness of their bedroom and then it seemed as if he did it because he couldn't help himself.

Now in the middle of the vast prairie, Diane shook her head. She'd been foolish to marry without love. Seth never once had said he loved her. She knew he had married her because he needed a wife. She groaned. Why had she even married him? What a mistake it had been! But she couldn't marry Bobby Ryder like she'd wanted.

She watched Bobby ride across the prairie toward her. He had seen her! Her love for him was as strong as it had been the day he returned the diary. As she peeked at him through her long lashes, she knew in her heart she couldn't marry him now even if she were free. The thought saddened her.

"Diane!" Smiling happily, Bobby reined in his horse and dropped to the ground. His skin was as dark as leather and his eyes as black as his hair. "I sure never expected to see you out here on a day like this!"

"Hello, Bobby," she managed to say without her voice trembling. She held her coat tightly to her. Could he hear the wild thump of her heart?

Bobby ran a gloved finger down her cheek.

Even through his glove she felt his special touch and her legs weakened.

"McGraw's a mighty lucky man. I'd give anything if you were mine."

Her pulse leaped. Why couldn't she tell him she felt the same way? She wanted to be his! But she couldn't be. She took a step back. How she longed to lean against him!

"I take it you're finally walking out on that worthless husband of yours."

Diane pulled away. "I am not! You know me better than that!"

"I only know you married Seth McGraw instead of me."

She weakened with longing, then faced him squarely. "You're not the marrying kind, Bobby."

"I could change. You could make me change."

She had thought the same thing, but when she'd almost given in to him, she realized that he would change her - for the worse. Reluctantly she drew further away from him so she couldn't feel the heat of his body. Just then a pain stabbed her. She gasped and sank down. He caught her and held her.

"What's wrong?"

She couldn't speak for a while, then gasped, "The baby." When the pain was gone she added, "I must get to Pa's."

Bobby frowned. "I'll take you." He picked her up as easily as if she was still thin and light and sat her side-saddle, then mounted behind the saddle. He circled her with his arms and caught up the reins as he nudged his horse forward.

She wanted to lean back against him, but sat straight and gripped the saddle horn with her right hand. She felt the heat of his body and smelled the leather of the saddle. If she turned her head even a little, she could kiss him. His arms tightened around her.

"Relax, Diane. I'm not going to bite you."

She wasn't afraid of what he'd do, but what she would do. Flushing, she looked off across the hills as the horse walked toward Pa's.

In the distance she saw smoke drifting up from the chimney of Pa's house. A cottontail hopped out of sight behind a tumbleweed. A hawk cried in the sky and swooped down for the rabbit, but flew away without it.

The horse rounded a low hill and Diane saw the one-story white frame house that sprawled across the yard and the tall red barn with naked cottonwood trees on the north side. She'd been born in the house when it was only four rooms and had lived there after Pa had added three more rooms until last year when she'd married Seth.

At the edge of the yard Bobby stopped his horse. "I'll leave you here so I don't get a lecture from your pa."

"Thank you." She didn't want a lecture either. Pa didn't like Bobby's lifestyle and didn't want his children to associate with him.

Bobby eased Diane to the ground, smiled, tipped his hat, and rode away.

A long-haired brown dog barked and ran to meet Diane as she watched until Bobby was out of sight.

She patted the dog's head between his pointed ears just as another pain tightened across her. She gasped and clutched her abdomen. "Butch, get Pa!"

Butch looked up at her questioningly, then raced to the house, barking wildly. Morgan Clements stepped out onto the porch while slipping his arms into his coat sleeves. He was medium build with graying hair and dark eyes. "What's going on, feller?"

Diane shouted, "Pa! Help me."

Morgan gasped, then called over his shoulder, "Laurel, Diane's coming. She's on foot!"

Laurel grabbed her shawl and stepped onto the porch. She had graying brown hair and wide brown eyes. An apron covered her gray serge work dress. She pressed her hand to her throat. "In this weather? Something terrible must have happened."

Morgan ran across the yard to Diane. "What's wrong?"

"The baby," Diane said with a gasp as another pain hit her. She gripped Morgan's arm and pressed her forehead against him.

His nerves tightened. The baby wasn't due yet. He wanted to urge Diane to keep walking, but he didn't. He remembered the pains Rachel had suffered giving birth to Hadley, Diane, Worth, and the baby who'd died, taking Rachel's life too. Then he'd married Laurel and she'd given birth to four children. Giving birth was painful and he wouldn't hurry Diane. Finally the pain ended and he helped her across the yard and up on the porch.

Laurel pulled Diane close, then led her inside. The kitchen was a large room with a cookstove giving off heat. Water boiled in a heavy teakettle. An oblong oak table stood at the side of the kitchen with eight chairs around it. The smell of freshly baked bread filled the room. Laurel eased Diane into a chair and helped her take off her coat and bonnet and heavy shoes. She handed Morgan the coat and bonnet to hang on the pegs near the back door and beside the washstand. Laurel rubbed Diane's hand. "When did you have the last pain?"

Struggling against tears, Diane sat at the kitchen table and looked out the window across the Nebraska prairie. It was as bleak as her heart. "A minute ago."

"Just as I got to her," Morgan said, pacing the kitchen nervously.

"When did the pains start?" Laurel asked as she rubbed Diane's cold hands.

"Early this morning." Her eyes wide, Diane clung to Laurel's hands. "I thought it was false labor, but I don't think so now."

Laurel looked over her shoulder at Morgan. "Get the doc."

Morgan nodded and hurried out. It took half an hour to get to town, so he knew he'd have to hurry. He didn't want Laurel to deliver the baby alone even though he knew she could if need be.

Laurel pulled Diane against her and prayed, "Heavenly Father, thank you for watching over Diane and this new baby. Help Diane to have an easy, quick delivery. In Jesus' name. Amen." Laurel kissed the top of Diane's head, then smiled. "You go in by the fire in the front room and relax in the rocking chair. The children will be home soon." The *children* were eighteen year-old Alane, sixteen year-old Maureen, twenty-one year-old Garrett, twenty year-old Forster, and of course, Worth who was hoping the baby would be born January 24 on his twenty-fourth birthday. "They rode into town in the buggy to bring Alane home. She's been teaching school the past few days."

Diane started to speak, but another pain seized her and she cried out. Maybe Pa wouldn't make it back in time with the doctor.

CHAPTER 2

In Broken Arrow Seth McGraw reached to untie the reins from the hitchrail when he heard someone shout his name. It was getting onto dark and he wanted to get home. He'd been at Nick Stone's place, but had to come and get more wood to finish building the buggy he'd started for Nick. Shivering even in his sheepskin coat, Seth turned and saw Bobby Ryder stumbling down the wooden sidewalk outside the saloon, drunk as usual when he was in town. His jaw set, Seth forced himself to nod. Bobby was the last person he wanted to see. He started to climb into the wagon.

Bobby lurched down the wooden sidewalk and fell against Seth's wagon. "That wife of yours is about to have my baby," Bobby laughed. "You know that, don't you, McGraw?"

Seth knotted his fists. He'd known all along the baby was Bobby's, but he'd never told Diane. Just before they were married, Bobby had cornered him at a school social and told him in great detail the fun he'd had with Diane. Seth had punched Bobby, sending him sprawling to the floor, then had walked out. He never told Diane what the fight was about and she never asked. He considered backing out of the wedding, but knew he couldn't. It would humiliate Diane too much - and himself too, for that matter. He'd gone off alone to pray for strength to go on with the marriage. Only God's strength had kept him sane.

Chuckling, Bobby stepped closer to Seth. "You see if that baby has my black hair or your red hair."

Anger surged through Seth and he slammed his fist into Bobby's leering face, sending him sprawling to the frozen ground. "Don't say another word, Bobby!" His face dark with rage, Seth climbed in the wagon and slapped the reins against the team. Bobby's words rang in his head over the clop of the hoofbeats and the creak of the wagon. He shouldn't have married Diane! But when she dared him to kiss her and he did, he was lost. He had loved her for as long as he could remember. He'd dreamed about her becoming his wife, sharing his home, bearing his children. She had loved him too until Bobby Ryder had pulled the dirty trick with her diary. Bobby had stolen the diary from Diane's desk, read it, then hid it in the woodpile. He told Seth what he'd done, laughing all the while. When Mr. Kurtis insisted Diane's diary be returned to her, Seth had decided to get it for her even if Bobby beat him senseless. At noon recess he found it in the woodpile, smiling as he thought of what Diane would say when he returned it to her. She might even give him a kiss. He had flushed with pleasure at the pure delight a kiss from Diane would give him. He started to walk away from the woodpile just as Bobby ran to him.

"Give that here!" Bobby grabbed the diary and ran to Diane.

Seth had raced after Bobby, but he was too late. Bobby was standing facing Diane and Kate. Seth had gritted his teeth and doubled his fists.

"Seth McGraw hid it, but I got it back for you," Bobby

had said.

Diane had hugged the diary to her and from that minute on had loved Bobby.

Seth groaned as the wagon swayed. He should've told Diane the truth then and fought Bobby if need be. But he hadn't. Now it was foolish to bring it up.

At first he had wondered why she married him, but after what Bobby said, he knew. She was going to have Bobby's baby and he wouldn't marry her. Seth gritted his teeth and slapped the reins against the horses. Diane had chosen to marry him because he had a ranch of his own and it was near her family. She would never move far from them.

Seth looked across the gray hills and forced back a cry of agony. When she told him she was expecting a baby, he'd stormed out of the house and ridden deep into the prairie. Finally he prayed for help, for added strength. He prayed for strength to keep from killing Bobby. He prayed for help to continue loving Diane. He prayed that he wouldn't run away to Oregon to live with his ma and pa and forget the life behind him. God had answered. His love for Diane continued and he had not killed Bobby.

Seth hunched inside his heavy sheepskin coat and groaned. Would the baby have Bobby's black hair or Seth's red hair?

Diane slowly opened her eyes. The kerosene lamp on the dresser cast a soft glow over the room. Voices drifted in from the front room along with the smell of coffee. Had Seth come yet? She lifted her head from the pillow Alane had embroidered with flowers and a butterfly and looked down at the sleeping baby in her arms. Her heart swelled with pride and happiness. He was beautiful! His name was

Morgan Clements McGraw just as she and Seth had decided if she had a boy. He had a mass of dark hair and he looked like Pa. Doc had arrived just in time to deliver the baby, much to Ma's relief. Diane was just glad to have the baby come and be done with the pain.

Just then Alane poked her head into the room. She was petite and looked younger than her eighteen years. Her brown hair curled onto her shoulders. It was her room, but she'd given it up for Diane and the baby. She was sleeping in Maureen's room. "Are you awake?"

Diane smiled, "Yes." The baby made little sucking noises and Diane laughed. "Listen to him, Alane! He's so precious!" Diane pushed her face against the baby's head. She'd already forgotten the pain she had suffered.

Pulling her yellow flannel robe closed over her nightdress, Alane touched the baby's red cheek. "Seth will be proud of him."

Diane didn't know about that, but she knew she was proud enough to pop off all her buttons. Even her anger at Seth had disappeared on seeing the wonderful baby they'd produced together. "I hope Seth comes soon. I can't wait for him to see Mor."

"Mor? Is that what you'll call him?"

Diane nodded. "Seth and I agreed on a nickname so nobody would call him Little Morgan all his life." Suddenly she wanted Seth beside her. She had done the right thing by marrying Seth! Why had she thought differently? He was the most wonderful man in the world because he'd given her Mor! "I wish Seth would hurry!"

Alane was glad to hear that. Sometimes she wondered if something was wrong between Seth and Diane. Obviously she'd been wrong. She carefully sank to the edge of the bed. "He might not make it tonight. It started to snow a while ago."

Diane sighed in disappointment, then she brightened. "He'll really be surprised to see the baby. I believe he'll think Mor's beautiful, don't you?"

"Of course! You already saw how Pa felt. Seth will be even more excited." Her brown eyes glowing, Alane touched Mor's cheek. "Diane, I want a baby too!"

"You have to get married first," Diane said with a laugh.

"I know." Alane sighed heavily and crossed her arms. "Sometimes I wonder if I'll ever find a husband." Her cheeks turned apple red. "I won't marry a cowboy! But they're the only men around who aren't already married."

"Don't be in a rush to marry. Enjoy your life the way it is, Alane. I didn't get married until I was twenty-four. I survived being called an old maid."

Alane lifted her chin. "I won't wait until I'm that old! I mean it, Di! I just might answer an ad and be a mail-order bride."

"What?" Diane jerked up, startling the baby, then settled back down. "Do Ma and Pa know what you're thinking?"

"No. And I don't want you telling them." Alane clasped her hands and leaned down toward Diane. "Please, Di. Promise you won't tell."

Diane saw the determination in Alane's face. She wanted to convince Alane to forget the foolish idea, but knew her sister could be very stubborn. "I promise. But don't do anything without talking to me first." Diane gripped Alane's hand. "Promise?"

Alane reluctantly nodded her head. She already had a letter written to a rancher in South Dakota who'd advertised in the newspaper for a mail-order bride. But she wouldn't send her letter for a while. Maybe a man would come riding on a big white stallion and carry her away. She could dream, couldn't she?

Mor squeaked and moved.

Diane laughed softly. "I hope he wakes up."

"Maybe I should put him in his basket so you can get some sleep."

"I don't want to give him up yet."

Alane laughed softly. "You'll have him all your life."

"I know." Diane yawned and her eyelids fluttered. "I reckon you better put him in his basket so I can sleep. I feel tired all at once."

Alane carefully picked Mor up and held him close. He felt soft and warm in his white gown and flannel blanket. She kissed his cheek and gently laid him on his stomach in the wicker clothes basket. It had been padded with a white flannel blanket and covered with a white muslin sheet. She covered him with a blanket Maureen had handstitched for the baby. The room was chilly, but they were all used to sleeping in a cold room.

"He's precious, isn't he?" Diane whispered.

"Yes." Alane brushed at a tear caught on her lashes.

"I wish Seth would come." The need to see Seth almost overwhelmed her. "I want him to see his baby."

"He will. You go to sleep now and if Seth comes, I'll bring him in."

Diane glanced toward the chest where Alane always kept her clock, but it wasn't there. "What time is it?"

"About nine." Alane turned the lamp low, but didn't blow it out. "Ma said she'll come check on you later, so don't try to get up without her help."

"I won't. I feel too weak." Diane watched Alane walk out, then sank down on her pillow. A picture of Seth smiling at her flashed across her mind. Suddenly she felt too wide awake and excited to lie still. Carefully she swung her feet to the cold wooden floor just inches from the basket and sat on the edge of the bed. She felt weak and sore, but she couldn't lie down a minute longer. "Where is Seth? He should've come."

Just then the door opened and Seth walked in, his wide-brimmed hat in his hands, his sheepskin coat hanging open. He smelled like cold, fresh air. His hair was a bright spot in the room. He saw Diane sitting on the edge of the bed and heard the little noises from the baby in the basket. He wanted to turn and run for fear the baby did indeed have black hair instead of red, but he had to make sure Diane was all right.

"Seth!" Smiling, Diane held her hand out to him without getting up. Oh, but she was glad to see him!

His heart leaped. She seemed genuinely pleased to see him. Part of him wanted to take her in his arms, but the other part cried out in anger at what she'd done. He managed to say, "Are you all right?"

She nodded, feeling let down that he didn't pull her close and kiss her. "I was worried about you, though, when you weren't here just after dark."

"I got home late." Because he didn't want to face her he'd done the chores before going inside. It had been long after dark before he found her note. He had considered not going after her, then decided he had to. She was his wife, after all. He never dreamed she'd had the baby. When Morgan had told him at the door, he almost turned and ran. It was hard to hold back his hurt and anger.

Diane laughed softly. "I tried to wait for you before I had the baby, but I just couldn't! He was very determined to be born."

"Is he...healthy?" He really wanted to ask if he was Bobby's baby.

"Yes! But he's tiny because he came early." Diane held her hand out to Seth. "Come look at him. He's beautiful!"

Seth hesitated, then took her hand. His pulse leaped just as it always did at her touch, but he didn't let it show. If she knew how much he loved her, she would take even more advantage of him than she already had.

She stood beside him at the basket. She waited for Seth's response. It puzzled her that he wouldn't turn back the blanket and look at Mor. "Pick him up and hold him."

His insides felt like a chunk of ice. "I might hurt him."

"You won't." She leaned against Seth and looked in his face. "I told Doc we'd chosen Morgan Clements McGraw as a name for him and to put it on the birth certificate."

"That's good." Thankfully she hadn't named him Bobby.

Diane touched Seth's arm. She felt him tense and wondered about it. "I want you to hold him and look at him. He's so tiny and precious!"

Seth bent down to lift the baby, then his hands froze in place. The baby did have dark hair! Seth's stomach tightened and he stepped away from Diane and away from the basket. He wanted to shout in anger and break something. He wanted to turn and run. "I can't touch him."

Diane frowned. "He won't break."

Seth struggled to control his anger and his great agony. He had so much wanted Mor to have red hair. Seth managed to say around the lump in his throat, "Get back in bed and rest. I'll see you tomorrow."

Tears pricked her eyes. "Why can't you stay? You can sleep here with me."

But he knew he couldn't. It would take another miracle from God for him to share a bed with her again as long as he lived. She had broken his heart. The proof was in the basket beside the bed. "I'll see you tomorrow," he said sharply.

She reached for his hand, but he strode out, closing the door with a snap. Weakly she sank down on the bed. Mor had made a difference in her feelings for Seth, but not in his feelings for her. He was indeed sorry they were married and sorry they had a baby!

Slowly she slipped back in bed and pulled the covers to her chin. She shivered even though she was warm.

Outdoors Seth mounted his horse and rode away in a swirl of snow. He leaned low over the saddle, his pain so great he couldn't sit up. How could he survive knowing Bobby was the baby's father?

Alone on the road that stretched on through the prairie, Seth lifted his head and cried with an anguish deep inside, "God, help me! I need your help worse than I've ever needed it before!" From the time he was a boy Seth had trusted God to help him in every situation. God always answered but this seemed different. It seemed impossible.

"No!" Seth shook his head as his horse raced on. "God, nothing is impossible with you. Nothing! You can heal my broken heart. You can help me forgive Diane and love her as a husband should love his wife."

As he prayed, a peace filled him. He knew he could accept Diane back when she returned. Back as a true wife? His stomach knotted. "Nothing is impossible with God!"

The next afternoon Diane awoke from a nap to find her friend Kate Mayberry kneeling beside the basket admiring Mor. The smell of baking bread drifted across the pleasantly warm room. Kate's long black hair hung down on her green wool dress. She was slender and pretty, but with a nose too long for her face.

Diane lifted her head and smiled, "Kate. Hi."

Her brown eyes sparkling, Kate looked up from the baby. "Di, he's the most adorable baby I've ever seen!"

"Thank you. I think so too." Laughing, Diane flipped back her blonde braids, eased out of bed, and slipped on a pink robe. "I'm glad you came."

Alarmed, Kate reached for Diane. "Should you be out of bed?"

"I'm fine. Only a little sore."

Kate relaxed and smiled. "What does Seth think of the baby?"

"He's afraid to touch him." Diane hadn't told even Kate why she'd married Seth, nor how unhappy she was.

"Seth's afraid?" Kate lifted her dark brows almost to her dark fringe. "I'm surprised. He loves kids!"

Diane stiffened. She knew that by watching him with children of all ages. But she dare not think it was only Mor he wouldn't touch. "Mor is tiny. Five pounds."

A wistful look on her face, Kate looked down at the baby, then at Diane. "I envy you, Diane. I want a baby too."

Diane squeezed Kate's hand. "You will."

"I don't think I'll ever get married." Kate lowered her voice even though she knew Garrett was in the barn helping his pa. "I love Garrett and he doesn't even notice me."

"My little brother is thinking of work." Diane knew

Kate had loved Garrett for an entire year now even though she was three years older than he was. Garrett liked Kate as a friend, but it never occured to him to think of her as a wife. "In the spring he's moving to his own homestead south of ours. He's excited about it."

Kate clasped her hands to her heart. "His own place! Maybe then he'll realize he needs a wife."

"Maybe." Diane didn't think so since Garrett would be busy from dawn to dark putting in fences and having a windmill put in. And he had to help Pa with the spring roundup, then drive his share of the herd to his place. He was going to be very busy indeed.

"What time is Seth coming today?"

"I don't know." Diane turned away and sank down in the rocking chair to hide the sudden tears in her eyes. She didn't know if Seth was coming. She'd prayed for him and for their marriage after he left last night. It had taken her a long time to fall asleep.

Mor whimpered and opened his eyes.

Kate cried out happily and knelt beside the basket. "Let me hold him, Di. Please!"

Diane laughed, "Go right ahead. But I'll have to nurse him soon. He gets hungry soon after he wakes up."

Kate gently picked Mor up and held him close. "He doesn't look like Seth much, does he?"

"No. He looks more like Pa."

"He has a perfect nose," Kate laughed. "I can't imagine a baby having my nose."

Mor whimpered, then cried lustily.

"He can't wait any longer." Diane reached for Mor. "Maybe the next one will have red hair like Seth's."

"A girl with Seth's hair," Kate sighed as she sank down

on the bed. "She'd be gorgeous!"

Diane nursed Mor while she and Kate talked more about children and their looks, then about a dress Kate was making as well as the latest town gossip.

Kate leaned forward. "I heard Macee Cannon - I mean Macee Caulder is coming back to town."

Diane gasped in shock. She and Macee had never gotten along. "Why? She didn't leave her husband, did she?"

"No. He died - was gored by a bull. They have a three year-old son named Barney."

"I wonder what she's going to do? Will she stay with her parents?"

"I guess so." Kate brushed her hair off her flushed cheek. "She used to like Seth."

Diane wrinkled her nose, "I remember."

"Did you know she used to sneak out with Bobby Ryder?"

Diane's heart stood still. She thought Bobby had gone out only with her until two years ago when she stopped seeing him because of his wild ways. "Where'd you ever hear that?" she asked sharply.

"From several people. I saw them together myself."

"I never knew that."

"Some folks say little Barney is Bobby's. They say Macee married Barney Caulder because Bobby wouldn't marry her."

Diane felt hot, then cold. Was it true? "Please, let's not gossip any more. It's too upsetting." She knew the gossiping wasn't bothering her, but it was what Kate was saying about Bobby and Macee. Could it be true? She knew Bobby went out with women after she stopped seeing him, but she'd never thought he did while they were together.

Kate grinned. "I am trying to stop gossiping altogether, but it's hard. What else is there to say?"

Diane laughed, "I suppose we could talk about recipes."

Kate wrinkled her nose, then smiled. "When will you go home?"

"In a week, I reckon. Ma knows when I go home I'll work too hard."

"I wish I could help you, but I must cook for Pa with Ma off visiting Drake in Omaha."

"I'll be fine. One of my sisters will come help me if I need help."

"Is Alane going to teach school the rest of the year?"

"Yes. Miss Dodge ran off with a traveling salesman," Diane laughed. "I never would've expected her to do such a thing."

"She wasn't very attractive. She probably had to take any man she could get."

"Probably," Diane sighed. What would she have done if Seth hadn't married her? Would she still be an old maid? What a terrible thought!

They talked a while longer, then Kate said goodbye. Diane burped Mor, changed his diaper, and put him back in the basket just as Laurel walked in with a glass of milk and slice of fresh bread for Diane. Laurel's flowered apron covered her green gingham dress. Gray strands of hair feathered out from the bun at the nape of her neck.

Smiling, Laurel set the small white plate and tall glass on a table beside the rocker. "Time for a snack, honey."

"Thanks, Ma." Diane sank down in the rocking chair and drank the milk and nibbled on the bread. "Do you know what I'd like?"

"Hot chocolate. You always loved it."

Diane laughed, "Not this time. I'd like you to play a song on the piano. I've missed your playing more than anything else since I left."

Laurel kissed Diane. "I'll play a while, then I want to talk to you."

Diane sighed, "You might as well talk first."

"You always did want to get unpleasant things out of the way first."

"I still do."

Laurel leaned against the tall footboard on the bed. "I want to know what's wrong between you and Seth."

Diane sat very still. "What makes you ask that?"

"I know you, honey. I've been your mother for twenty-one years. Now, talk to me."

Diane ran a finger around the rim of her empty glass. She was quiet a long time. "Seth doesn't love me."

"I can't believe that."

Diane laughed, "Ma, I'm your child, and you want to think everyone loves me. It's just not true."

"But I've seen the way he looks at you and have heard how he talks about you."

"He's different at home when no one's around. He ignores me. He gets angry."

"That doesn't sound like Seth. I've known him all of his life. Your pa and I love him as much as our own sons."

Diane swallowed hard. "He wouldn't even hold Mor. He doesn't want a baby. And I was sure he would."

"It takes some men a while to get used to having a baby."

"I suppose so," Diane bit her lip. She knew it was more than that with Seth, but she couldn't imagine what.

"Be patient with him. Give him lots of love and care."

Diane nodded. She'd never given him love, but she had

met his needs as much as she could.

They talked a while longer, then Laurel played several hymns on the piano. Diane leaned back in the chair and closed her eyes. She remembered how upset she'd been when Laurel first played Ma's piano. Now the piano was as much Laurel's as it had been Ma's.

Diane drifted off to sleep, then awoke at a sound in the room. Seth and Laurel stood beside the basket, looking down at Mor. Seth's shirt was wrinkled and his levis needed washing. His red hair was combed neatly and he looked as if he'd just shaved. Was he getting enough to eat? Was he working too hard? He looked tired.

Laurel picked up Mor and laid him in Seth's arms before he knew what she'd planned.

Diane held her breath as she watched the stricken look on Seth's face. Was he afraid of Mor? The baby looked very tiny next to Seth.

He wanted to push the baby back into Laurel's arms, but he forced himself to hold him. Seth looked into the tiny red face at the little nose and wide mouth. Perfect eyebrows were arched above his eyes closed in sleep. His ears were perfect - like miniature ears. He moved his tiny fist and Seth smiled. Love sparked in his heart and grew. He bent his head and kissed Mor's soft cheek.

Tears filled Diane's eyes and she quickly brushed them away. Seeing Seth and Mor together touched her deeply. Maybe she could learn to love Seth as much as Ma loved Pa. It was hard to imagine loving anyone - even Bobby Ryder - that much. She frowned. Why had she thought that? She loved Bobby more than Ma loved Pa. Didn't she?

Laurel glanced over and noticed Diane was awake. "We didn't mean to wake you, Diane."

Seth turned, feeling awkward holding Mor with Diane looking on. "He's a fine baby." His voice sounded strained in his ears. Would Diane and Laurel notice?

"I know," Diane said softly. "I'm glad you think so too."

"I must fix the fire." Smiling, Laurel walked out, closing the door behind her.

Diane slowly stood, tying the pink robe securely. She suddenly wished she was as slender as she'd been before Mor. Would Seth think she was fat and ugly?

Seth couldn't think of anything to say. Diane looked fragile and tired. "Shouldn't you be in bed?"

"I'm fine." She stepped close to Seth and looked into Mor's sleeping face. Finally she smiled at Seth. "We're parents now. Doesn't it seem strange? But nice," she quickly added.

Seth's heart jerked. He was a parent. The baby bore his name and would live in his house. That made him more a father to the baby than Bobby Ryder! "I'll be a good papa to Mor."

His words sounded like a solemn vow. Did he think she didn't expect him to be a good father? "I know you will. And I'll be a good momma."

Mor opened his eyes and waved his fists in the air.

Seth chuckled, "He's real. It's hard to imagine he's a real person since he's so small."

"He's real and he's ours," Diane smiled, then the smile froze at the look on Seth's face. What had she said that hurt him? She glanced at him again and the look was gone. Maybe she was wrong. Everything was going to be just fine. It had to be!

CHAPTER 3

Diane stood on the porch and breathed the crisp, cold air deeply into her lungs. A cow mooed in the corral beside the barn. Seth hadn't come to see her or Mor since the day after Doc had circumcised Mor. Seth said he had to finish the buggy for Nick Stone. In the winter Seth built buggies to bring in cash money. The rest of the year he was busy raising cattle and horses and the feed to keep them through the winters.

Just then Worth walked up the steps, his slant-heeled leather boots covered with fresh snow. He looked warm in his sheepskin-lined leather jacket. He had the same blonde hair and blue eyes as Diane and was a year younger. "What're you doing out here?" Worth asked with a frown. "I thought you were supposed to stay in bed."

"I needed fresh air." Diane looked at the snowdrifts around the house. Her eyes sparkled as she looked up at Worth and giggled, "Want a snowball fight?"

Worth laughed, "Sure. Next month, maybe." He sobered and studied her. "Is something wrong?"

She caught his hand with both of hers. She'd always mothered Worth when he was a sickly child, then continued to be close to him when he'd finally grown healthy and strong. He was taller than Pa and as strong as Hadley, their older brother, and better-looking than both. "Worth, sometimes I think I'd like to stay here forever."

He frowned slightly, "Something wrong between you and Seth?" Worth loved Seth like a brother and he didn't want to see any problems between the two of them.

Diane wanted to pour out her heart to Worth, but she held back. She didn't want any of her family to know why she'd married Seth. She felt guilty enough as it was at what she'd done. She smiled hesitantly. "We had a lot of fun here. I know we worked hard, but we had fun too."

"We sure did." Pushing his gray, wide-brimmed hat to the back of his head, Worth looked off toward the snow-covered hills. "I love the family and I like living here but, Diane, sometimes I have an urge to go back east where Grandma and Grandpa first came from."

Diane's heart zoomed to her feet. How could she survive without Worth living nearby? "To live?" she whispered.

"Maybe. I don't know. I want to see more than these Nebraska hills and this endless prairie. I want to feel more than the Nebraska wind in my face. I want to walk among a crowd of folks and not know a one of them!"

"Not me! I like knowing everybody." Diane bit her lip. "I never knew you felt like this."

"It's been building up inside me."

"Why didn't you tell me?"

"Your mind's been full of the baby."

"I know." She gripped his hand with both of hers. "I'm sorry. I didn't mean to forget about everyone else."

Worth shrugged. "I might go visit Hadley and Maple before spring round-up."

"Oh, I wish I could go with you to see Hadd! I miss him so much! Ma gave me their letter to read. They sound very happy." Diane's heart lurched. Why couldn't she and Seth be happy? Hadd and Maple had married without love, then had fallen in love afterward. Could it work that way with her and Seth?

"I wish I could've been there to help Hadd add on to the house. With the money he made from training and selling horses he was able to add three big rooms."

"And they planted more fruit trees. I think I'll plant apple trees in the spring. Seth should like that."

"Spoken like a true wife," Worth sighed heavily as he leaned against the porch railing. He slowly pulled off his gloves and pushed them into his pockets. "I'd like to have a wife, but I don't know a single girl I could love enough. Maybe I'll bring a bride back from the east."

"A greenhorn?" Diane's eyes widened in shock. "How can a tenderfoot survive Nebraska?"

Worth nodded, "You're right. It was a dumb idea." He grinned. "I could marry Ganny Blake." She was almost 70 years-old and worked at the newspaper office with her brother. "She comes the closest to what I want in a woman."

"She's full of spunk, all right. Have you heard she wants to go around the world like Nellie Bly, that newspaper woman from New York?"

"She told me. I said I'd go with her."

"Oh, Worth!"

"I know. I shouldn't leave the family. In a few days I'll be twenty-four years-old. What have I done besides work the ranch and go to school? Nothing! What have I seen besides this?" He waved his arm to take in the area around him. "I can't settle down to more of the same like you and Hadley. And like Garrett and Forster are planning to do. Forster said he might get a homestead at the edge of the sandhills near Hadley."

"That'd be nice for Hadley, but sad for us to have him that far away." It took a long time to drive the buggy the fifty miles to Hadley's place. "If I could, I'd keep everybody here in a tight little circle."

"I know you would." Worth pulled his hand free and pushed his fingers into the back pockets of his levis. "But I can't be kept in a tight circle, Di. Not yet at least."

They talked a while longer, then Diane said, "Did you know Macee's back?"

Worth flushed. In eighth grade he'd thought he would marry her even if she was a couple of years older. But she had fallen for Bobby like all the other girls. She turned wild after she graduated from eighth grade, and he stopped caring for her. He refused to court a girl with low standards. He wouldn't marry a girl who didn't know Jesus as her personal Savior. He wouldn't even court one who didn't. "What's Macee going to do?"

"Kate said she'll stay home with her parents. She has a three year-old boy named Barney after her dead husband."

"I sure thought she'd snag Bobby Ryder, especially when she...you know. She sure did love him."

Diane's heart froze. Here it was again - Bobby and Macee. Was it true? Would she have to admit to herself that Bobby hadn't cared for her enough to be faithful to her? Ma always said that if a man couldn't be faithful before the wedding, he wouldn't be after. Diane thrust the thought aside and turned her attention back to Worth. "You won't court Macee now that she's back, will you?"

"Not if she was the only woman alive!"

Diane breathed a sigh of relief.

"I heard around town a few days ago that Bobby Ryder's been gambling again. I heard he lost a lot of money to that gambler, Julius Goddard."

Diane frowned. "Gambling's not allowed in Broken Arrow! I thought the sheriff ran Goddard out of town."

"So did I, but he's still there." Worth shook his head in disgust. "You'd think Bobby would know not to gamble. But he always was looking for trouble. I never could understand how you could be seen with him."

Diane flushed, "He wasn't always as bad as he is now."

"Sure he was! Remember how he lied to you about Ma's diary?"

Diane stiffened, "Lied to me?"

"He said Seth took the diary and hid it. Actually, Seth found it where Bobby hid it and was all set to give it back to you when Bobby grabbed it from him."

Diane sagged weakly against Worth. Bobby had taken the diary! Bobby had lied!

"Easy, Di!" Worth wrapped an arm around her. "I knew you shouldn't be up. Let me help you inside."

In a daze Diane leaned against Worth as he walked her through the warm kitchen smelling of coffee and the front room to Alane's bedroom where Mor was sleeping soundly.

"Are you all right?" Worth asked as he tugged off her

coat and eased her down in the rocker.

"I need to rest," she whispered. She gripped the arms of the maple rocker as she watched Worth pull off her boots and walk out, closing the door softly. A sob tore at her throat. Bobby, not Seth, had stolen her diary! Worth wouldn't make up such a story. Her love for Bobby had flamed into life because of the diary. What of the love now? She whimpered and helplessly shook her head. She'd dreamed for years of marrying Bobby all because of the diary. Suddenly she felt empty inside. Had the feelings been make-believe? Did she still love him? She frowned. Of course she did! She wasn't so shallow that she would stop loving him because of what Worth had said. "And what Kate said," Diane muttered, then clamped her hand over her mouth. Maybe she should stay. Seth might not care if she came home or not.

Mor made funny little noises and cried a short cry, the way he always did when he was first waking up to be fed.

Diane pushed aside thoughts of Bobby and Seth as she walked to the basket for Mor. Her legs still felt weak and her insides quivered. Her whole life suddenly felt off kilter.

She changed Mor, wrapped him in a dry, blue flannel blanket, and sat back in the rocker to nurse him. Just as she finished Maureen burst into the room, bringing in the smell of cold air. At sixteen she was self-assured and planned to be a newspaper woman like Nellie Bly. Maureen brushed back her long dark hair and tugged her green wool dress in order. Her brown eyes sparkled with excitement.

"Diane, I talked to Ganny Blake today! You will never in your wildest dreams guess what she's going to do!"

Diane laughed and shook her head, "Travel around the world the way Nellie Bly did?"

Maureen's face fell, "Who told you?"

"Kate, I think."

Maureen shrugged, "No matter." Her eyes flashed and she clasped her hands together. "Ganny wants me to go with her!"

"What?" Diane cried, making Mor jerk at the sudden noise. "You can't go! You're a baby!"

Maureen scowled at Diane. "Don't say that! Just because I'm the youngest in the family doesn't make me a baby! I will be seventeen next month! Lots of girls are married by then."

Diane shook her head. "Ma and Pa won't let you go."

"Don't say that!" Maureen flung up her hands. "Why can't I do what I want? I might even get to meet President Harrison. Or Vice-President Morton. Besides, Ganny will pay my way. She needs me to go with her to help her. She's not a young woman, you know."

"But it's so dangerous!"

Maureen knelt by the rocker and looked into Diane's face with wide brown eyes. "Nellie Bly did it and she was younger than you. She was safe. She went by train and ship and coach. It took her 72 days, 6 hours, and 11 minutes. She didn't get hurt or lost or anything. I want to do the same thing! I want to see the places Nellie Bly wrote about and I want to write about them!"

Giant tears welled up in Diane's eyes. "Hadd moved

away and Forster might. Worth's talking about going back east, and now you!" And even Alane was talking about being a mail-order bride, but Diane didn't say anything about that. "What's happening to this family? We should all stay together! I can't bear to have us apart!"

Her face flushed, Maureen jumped up and paced the room in quick, short strides. Finally she stopped and looked down at Diane, "Why did you say that? Children are supposed to leave their parents and go out on their own! Not all of us want to be babied like you do!"

Diane gasped, "Babied? What do you mean by that?"

Maureen dropped down beside Diane again. "Don't get upset, Di. But you know you like Ma babying you. You always have. Sometimes I think you're sorry you married Seth and wish you'd stayed home instead. Even if it meant you'd be an old maid."

Diane helplessly shook her head.

"I think you should be the youngest in the family, then you'd get all the babying you need."

Moaning, Diane buried her face in Mor's soft blue blanket. How could Maureen be so mean to her? "Don't say anymore, Maureen," Diane whispered.

Maureen jumped up. "See what I mean? You can't talk to me! You hide your head and pout!"

Her blue eyes flashing with anger, Diane lifted her head. Her eyes were dry and her cheeks flushed. "I am not pouting! You hurt my feelings!"

Maureen tossed her head. "Oh, poo! You just don't like anyone to see your faults."

"Faults?" Diane's nerves tightened. How could her baby sister see faults in her?

"We all have them, Di." Maureen leaned back against the footboard of the bed. "Even I do. But I look at them and try to change. You won't even look."

"That's not true!"

"Look at the way you insisted on keeping company with Bobby Ryder when you knew Ma and Pa didn't want you to."

"They never told me that!"

"They did so! You just didn't listen. You were so sure he'd marry you, but we all knew he wouldn't. It took you a long time to realize it."

Diane felt almost too weak to hold Mor against her shoulder. She eased him down in the crook of her arm. "Why are you saying this now?"

"I've said it lots of times in the past, but you never listened - not to Ma and Pa and certainly not to me!"

"I suppose you don't think I'm good enough for Seth," Diane said in a small voice that trembled slightly.

"I know if I were married to Seth, I'd love him with my whole heart - not just pretend to love him. He's the most wonderful man I know!"

Diane felt as if she'd been kicked in the stomach. How could Maureen have seen into her heart to know she didn't love Seth? Had the others known all along the very thing she'd tried to keep a secret? It was almost too much to bear.

Maureen pushed herself away from the bed and lifted her chin high. "I suppose I'd better tell you what I'm going to do."

Diane's heart sank.

"I am going to expose that gambler, Julius Goddard, for the cheat he is. And by doing that, I'll expose Bobby

Ryder for what he is!"

"Maureen, what're you planning?" Diane cried in alarm.

"I can't tell you, but it'll make the headlines in the Broken Arrow News! See if it doesn't! Maybe then you'll see Bobby Ryder is a snake in the grass, a weasel in the chicken coop, a burr under the saddle, and...." Maureen frowned in thought. "And anything else bad that I can't think of right now!"

Diane went hot, then cold. "Why are you telling me?"

"Do you think I'm blind? I know you love Bobby Ryder."

"Maureen! How can you say that?" Diane trembled. "I married Seth."

"I know. And I know why. Bobby wouldn't marry you."

Diane sank back weakly. "Does anyone else in the family think that?"

Maureen shook her head. "I really don't know. I haven't said anything in case they don't know. They all think you're perfect. But I know you're not. Nobody is."

A tear ran down Diane's hot cheek. "Do you hate me?"

"Of course not! I love you!"

"Then why're you doing this to me?"

Maureen knelt beside Diane again. "I can love others even if I know their faults. I love you, Di. You're my big sister."

Diane sobbed softly. Maureen was not being nice at all. "I'm tired and want to be alone."

"Okay," smiling, Maureen jumped up and hurried to the door. "I'll talk to you later." She started out the door, then looked back, her eyes twinkling. "Don't feel sorry for yourself, Di. Look at your faults and ask the Lord to help you change." Maureen closed the door with a snap.

Diane gasped at Maureen's audacity. "How dare she talk to me that way?" Diane muttered as she carefully laid Mor down in the basket on his stomach. She picked up the hairbrush and brushed her hair in quick, angry strokes. Maureen always had thought too highly of herself.

Off and on the next few days Diane thought of what Maureen had said. Each time it made her feel sad, then angry. She tried to stay away from Maureen as much as possible. It was almost impossible because of the small house and having meals together around the big oval table in the kitchen.

One evening after the dishes were done Laurel and Diane were alone in the kitchen while the others sang around the piano in the front room. Laurel had taught them all how to play the piano when they were still young.

Diane hung the damp dishtowel to dry over the rack in back of the stove, then sat at the table. The kitchen was snug and warm even though the wind howled around the corners of the house. Smells of roast venison and onions still hung in the air.

Laurel pushed back her graying hair and sat next to Diane. "Honey, it's time for you to go home. If Seth doesn't come in the morning, Pa will take you and Mor home."

Diane's heart plunged to her feet. "I thought I could stay until after Worth's birthday."

"You and Seth can come over for the celebration." Laurel lifted Diane's hand and held it against her soft cheek. "I love you, honey, and I'll miss you and Mor. But you don't dare get so comfortable here that you won't want to go to your own home. It wouldn't be right for me to let you do that."

Diane bowed her head. "It's easier to stay here, Ma."

"I know. But Seth needs you and you need him. Go home where you belong. Let Seth get to know his son."

Diane wanted to say, "If he really wanted to know his son, he'd have made a greater effort to come over." But she said, "He doesn't seem very interested."

"He had to get the buggy finished for Nick. Seth explained that to us. It was hard for him to take care of his chores and go to Nick's to finish the buggy and make the trip here too. He's probably done by now, so you are going home in the morning no matter what."

"But I don't think I can take care of Mor all by myself."

"I could send Maureen home with you."

"No! No, I'll be all right, I suppose." Diane would never allow Maureen to stay with her no matter how badly she needed help.

Laurel frowned slightly, "Are you and Maureen having a tiff again?"

Diane shrugged, "She's not very nice to me."

"She is very outspoken. But she loves you. You must know that."

Diane didn't know any such thing. She decided it was wise to drop the subject of Maureen. "Seth will probably be able to help me a lot."

"Of course he will."

Later Diane walked to the bedroom and stood at the window. The moon was bright enough to cast shadows in the snow. A coyote sat at the crest of a hill with its nose raised to the moon. She couldn't hear the howl over the music in the front room. Finally she turned away and changed into her flannel nightdress. Alane would be glad to get her room back. Diane brushed at a tear as she slipped into bed. She had to go home no matter how she felt.

The next morning Laurel hugged Diane goodbye, kissed Mor, then covered his face. "Pa's waiting in the sleigh."

Diane struggled to hold back her tears. How hard it was to leave! She looked around the cozy kitchen. Breakfast dishes were stacked at the end of the table while water boiled on the stove. The boys were doing chores and Maureen had ridden to town with Alane. They had all said goodbye, but none of them seemed sad to see her leave.

Laurel opened the door and Diane stepped out. The wind was down and the sun was shining so brightly the snow almost blinded her. Bells on the harness jingled merrily as Pa drove the sleigh right up to the porch.

"It's a fine morning to ride home," Pa called from the sleigh.

"I'm coming, Pa." Diane kissed Laurel's cheek. "Come see us soon."

"We will," Laurel hugged Diane and Mor again. "God is always with you, Diane."

She nodded, then slowly walked off the porch to the

sleigh. She held Mor up to Pa, climbed into the sleigh, took the baby back, then pulled the lap robe up in place. The trip home was going to be much different than the trip to Pa's ranch. She thought of her time with Bobby and her cheeks burned.

"Relax, Diane," Morgan said softly as the horses walked down the snow-covered road. Steam floated back from their noses. The bells covered the sound of their hooves.

Diane leaned her head against Pa's arm. "It's kind of hard to go back."

"You've always been a home body. Seth's home will seem like your home again."

"I know." Diane looked into Pa's face. His skin was like leather from being out in all kinds of weather. "Was it hard for you to leave your parents?"

"A little, but I loved your ma so much I wanted to be with her more than anyone else. I thought it was the same with you and Seth."

"Yes," she said, flushing uncomfortably. She watched a herd of antelope run across the hill and disappear behind another. She didn't want to talk about Seth with Pa. He could see right through her.

"Diane, has Seth said anything about horse thieves?"

Her eyes widened. "No. Why?"

"I can't find a sorrel mare I bought from Powers Carson over in Boone County." Morgan shrugged. "The mare could be somewhere on the range, I reckon, but I haven't spotted her in the past two weeks since I've been looking for her. Neither have the boys."

"Do you think Seth has had horses stolen?"

"It happens that way. Rustling from neighboring

ranches."

Diane shivered even though she was warm. What if Seth tried to stop someone from stealing his stock? He could be killed! "Ask him when we get there."

Morgan nodded. "I will. I thought maybe he talked to you about it."

"He didn't." Pa had no idea Seth didn't talk to her about anything.

"I'll warn him to be on the lookout."

Diane nodded. And she'd talk to him about it too after Pa was gone. Seth could be too daring at times.

When they reached the ranch, Seth stood in the yard outside the house. He wore his warm coat and gloves. He seemed to be waiting for someone. Had he learned Pa was bringing her home?

Morgan reined in the team near Seth. "Howdy, Seth," Morgan said with a happy wave.

Seth glanced at Diane, then quickly away. He smiled at Morgan, "Glad to see you!" He forced himself to smile at Diane. "I hope you're well enough to come back."

"I am." Diane held Mor down to Seth.

He froze, then took the baby.

Diane climbed from the sleigh, but didn't take Mor back. It was about time Seth took a hand with tending their son.

"I have coffee on the stove, Morgan," Seth said as he fell into step beside Morgan who was carrying a pack of Diane's and Mor's clothes. "Can you come in a while?"

"Sure can."

Diane hung back and looked around at the big house and barn, the chicken house, the shed, the outhouse, and the sod house left from the bachelor who'd first lived here. Seth's parents had bought the place when the bachelor wanted to hunt for gold in South Dakota.

Seth stopped at the door and looked back at Diane, "You coming?"

She nodded and hurried after him. The house was warm inside, but didn't feel cozy like Pa's. Dirty dishes were piled on one end of the kitchen table. The scarred wooden floor was dirty from tracking in snow and dirt. The door to the back room stood open and she saw a pile of dirty clothes beside the neatly stacked wood.

Seth saw Diane taking in the room and he flushed. "I'm expecting someone to come clean."

Diane shrugged, "It doesn't matter. I can do it." She was used to hard work. Besides, it would keep her mind occupied so she wouldn't have to think about all the things churning away inside her.

"I didn't want you to come back to a dirty house."

"It doesn't matter," Diane said a little too sharply.

"Who'd you get to come clean?" Morgan quickly asked as he set the pack down and hung his coat over the back of a chair.

Seth hesitated, "Macee Caulder."

Diane froze, her arms half out of her coat. Macee! Diane's stomach knotted. And Seth hadn't known she was coming home today! He had planned to be here alone with Macee! How dare he? "I don't need *her* help."

Seth shook his head. "You can't take care of this place alone until you're stronger."

"How is it you hired Macee?" Morgan asked.

"I saw her in town yesterday and she was looking for

work. She doesn't want to be a burden on her folks."

"I bet," Diane muttered under her breath as she hung her coat on a peg near the back door.

Suddenly feeling at a loss, Seth looked down at Mor in his arms. "Shall I lay him in his cradle?"

"I will," Diane reached for Mor. Her hands brushed Seth's and a jolt went through her. Her cheeks red, she took Mor and hurried to the bedroom she and Seth had shared the past nine months. The big four-poster bed was unmade, but the rest of the room looked neat and clean. The cradle was made up with a clean sheet over the mattress. Carefully she laid Mor on his stomach in the cradle, then smiled down at him. Pa had made the cradle three months ago and she'd daydreamed about her baby sleeping in it. Now, here he was. She bent over the cradle and smiled as she gently stroked Mor's head.

Just then she heard a horse and sleigh drive up. She rushed to the window and pulled back the muslin curtains. It was Macee Caulder! She looked pretty in her white bonnet trimmed in red that matched her hair. A little boy dressed in warm clothes and covered with a robe sat beside her. "She brought her little boy! Just how long is she planning to stay?"

Her lips pressed tightly together, Diane watched Seth run to the sleigh and help Macee down. Did he hold her a little too long? He lifted the boy out and held him in his arms, laughing and talking to him. Seth wasn't afraid to hold little Barney like he had been with Mor!

Whirling about, Diane marched across the room, through the front room and into the kitchen. Her cheeks were flushed and fire shot from her eyes.

Morgan caught Diane's arm, "Easy, honey. Don't

54

tear into Macee the way you did when you were girls. You're not children any longer."

Diane took a deep, steadying breath. Pa was right. She would not toss Macee out. But Macee was not going to touch Seth's dirty clothes or the dirty dishes! Macee was not going to take over as the housewife of this house!

Her fists knotted at her sides, Diane watched the door for Seth and Macee.

CHAPTER 4

Steeling himself for the look Diane would give him, Seth stood Barney on the porch beside him and opened the door for Macee. His stomach tight with nerves, Seth followed Macee and Barney inside. "Macee, you remember Morgan Clements, don't you?" Seth forced his voice to stay normal. He should never have allowed Macee to talk him into working for him!

"Of course!" Macee smiled at Morgan and held her hand out for a firm handclasp.

Diane lifted her chin and forced a smile. Why had Seth asked Macee to work for him? "Hello, Macee."

"Hi, Diane," Macee smiled, but it didn't reach her blue eyes. "Congratulations on your baby boy."

"Thank you. Take her wrap, Seth, while I pour a cup of coffee for her." Diane wanted to make sure Macee knew she was the woman of this household. She turned to Barney and smiled. He had black hair and eyes and looked like Bobby Ryder. Diane's heart squeezed in pain, but she managed to turn to Pa and smile at him. "Pa, help Barney off with his coat, would you?"

"Sure," smiling, Morgan hunkered down to Barney. "So you're Barney. Did you like the ride out here?"

Barney grinned and nodded. "The bells jingled and jingled. Me and Ma sang lots of songs." He turned to Macee, "We did sing, didn't we, Ma?"

Smoothing down her burgundy wool dress, Macee smiled lovingly at her son, "We sure did." She turned to Seth. Wisps of strawberry blonde hair curled onto her cheeks and forehead. "He's quite a singer."

Barney stuck out his chest and sang two verses of "Billy Boy" before Macee stopped him.

Diane saw the pride in Macee's eyes and it surprised her. She'd thought Macee was too selfish to love anyone but herself. And Bobby Ryder, or so she'd been told. Abruptly she turned away and filled white mugs with coffee and a glass with milk for Barney. They sat at the table and talked about the weather, the new year, and the changes in Broken Arrow. Diane forced herself to enter the conversation even though she wanted to lock herself in the bedroom with Mor until Seth sent Macee away.

Much later Morgan pushed his coffee cup back and stood. His gray flannel shirt was tucked neatly into his levis and held in place with a wide leather belt. "Seth, show me the mare you've been working with, will you?"

Smiling, Seth jumped up. "Sure." His boots loud against the floor in the sudden silence, he grabbed his coat and hat. He needed to get away from the tension he felt in Diane. "That mare's a quick learner."

"Do you plan to sell her?" Morgan asked as they excused themselves and walked out, letting in a blast of cold air.

Diane clasped her hands in her lap. Now what? She didn't want to be alone with Macee.

"I'd like to see your baby," Macee said hesitantly.

"He's asleep, but you can look at him." Diane led the way to the bedroom. She wished she'd taken time to make the bed first, but she hadn't. She felt the blue ribbon that held back her blonde hair slipping and she tied it quickly.

Holding Barney's hand, Macee walked to the cradle and looked down at Mor. "He's so little! Look at the sweet baby, Barney."

He dropped on his knees beside the cradle and pushed his face down close to Mor's.

"Be gentle," Macee said softly.

Diane moved restlessly. What a tiny waist Macee had! But then her boy was three years-old, not three weeks. Diane bit the inside of her bottom lip. She had to say something, not just stand there like a lump. What could she say? "How much did Barney weigh when he was born?"

"Seven pounds," Macee turned to Diane. "Yours?"

"Five. He came early."

"I wondered."

Diane bristled. "What do you mean by that?"

Macee shrugged and looked very innocent. "Not a thing. Should I have?"

Diane bit back the sharp retort on the tip of her tongue. She knew good and well that every woman in the area counted the nine months when anyone got married and had her first baby. "Your little boy is adorable."

Macee beamed as she pulled Barney against her leg. "Thank you. I don't know what I'd do if I didn't have him."

"I'm sorry about the loss of your husband."

Macee shrugged, "I'll survive."

Diane glanced at the unmade bed and flushed. She had to get Macee out of the bedroom! "Shall we go back to the kitchen for another cup of coffee?"

"I'll make the bed first."

Diane gasped, "No!"

Macee tipped her head and studied Diane. "But I came to work for Seth. Or didn't he tell you?"

"He told me. But I don't need help. I'm home now and feeling strong."

"Don't be ridiculous!" Macee glanced at Barney where he stood looking out the window, then hurried to the bed and started pulling the sheet tight.

"Macee, leave the bed alone," Diane said sharply.

Macee frowned at Diane, then went right back to work.

Her face burning with shame, Diane hurried to the other side of the bed and pulled the sheets tight, then the blankets. They had the bed made in a couple of minutes. Diane wanted to grab Macee by the arm and march her out into a snowdrift.

Macee caught Barney's hand. "I'll do the dishes now. Diane, lie down and rest while I work."

"I'll do no such thing!" She followed Macee to the kitchen. "I thought you hated housework."

"Normally I do, but I'll like working for Seth."

Diane blocked Macee's way to the dishpan. "Don't think you can steal my husband away from me, Macee Cannon!"

Macee laughed and shook her head, "Don't worry about it, Diane Clements."

"McGraw!"

Macee shrugged. "And my name happens to be Caulder. Now that we have that settled, let me wash the dishes."

"I'll do it."

"Seth hired me and I'll do my job."

"You've always been stubborn, haven't you?"

"And you've always been a spoiled brat!"

Diane gasped and sank weakly to a chair. She watched Macee load dishes in the heavy dishpan. With a sharp paring knife she shaved the end of the bar of soap onto the dishes, then poured scalding hot water from the teakettle over the dishes. She filled the teakettle again from the bucket of water on the washstand and set it back on the stove to heat. She pushed a couple pieces of wood into the stove and closed the lid with a clank. Diane's muscles tightened at Macee's every movement.

"It's too late to heat water to do the wash, so I'll be back tomorrow morning early."

Her eyes flashing, Diane shook her head, "Don't bother. I'll do the wash."

With her hands on her waist, Macee faced Diane squarely. "Seth hired me and only he can fire me."

"Then I'll see that he does!"

"You should be thankful for the help. Are you that afraid you'll lose Seth to me just like you did Bobby?"

Diane's face flamed. Before she could answer, Barney ran to Macee with a cry. She settled him down as Diane pulled her anger in check. She realized the sooner Macee finished the work, the sooner she'd leave.

Macee carried Barney to the window and stood him down. "Watch for Seth while I do the dishes."

Barney pressed his nose against the windowpane and

watched for Seth.

Diane pushed herself up. She was tired, but would not let Macee know. "I'll help with the dishes."

Macee shrugged, "It's not worth arguing over." She washed and Diane rinsed and dried.

"I saw Kate Mayberry yesterday," Macee said as she poured more hot water in the dishpan. "It's too bad she's still an old maid."

"Maybe she likes it that way," Diane snapped.

Macee rolled her eyes. "I was only making an observation. You don't have to snap at everything I say, do you?"

"Kate is my best friend and I won't have you make such an observation! It would hurt her feelings."

"Only if you tell her I said it."

Diane rubbed a plate hard with the dishtowel and set it in the cupboard with a clatter. Macee was much worse than she'd been in school! There was no winning with her.

"I met that gambler, Julius Goddard, too." Macee shivered. "I didn't like him at all."

"Did you actually talk to him?"

Macee nodded, "I tried not to speak, but I was forced to. My pa was with him."

Diane's eyes widened. Jack Cannon was on the school board and he was against gambling as much as the rest of the board. "Why was your pa with him?"

Macee dropped the dishrag in the hot water and frowned. "I asked him later, but he wouldn't tell me. Ma is worried. She said she asked Roy Prescott why he hadn't run the man out of town."

"What'd the sheriff say?"

"He said he had, but Goddard came back and wasn't gambling, so he was free to stay."

Diane shook her head, "Do you believe he's not gambling?"

"No," Macee narrowed her eyes. "I know he's trouble. Especially for...for Bobby." She flushed.

Her eyes wide, Diane stared at Macee. "Do you...love Bobby?" It hurt Diane's throat to say the words.

Macee flushed, "No. Of course not! He's happy being a cowboy without a care in the world."

"He sure is!" Diane bit back a sigh.

In the barn Seth leaned against the stall door beside Morgan and looked at the sorrel mare he'd named Red Lightning. Pigeons cooed in the loft and a cat meowed near the door. "I hope you're wrong about horse thieves, Morgan."

"I don't think I am."

"Hang 'em high! That's what I say!" Seth flushed even as he said it. It wasn't like him to be violent.

"That's what'll happen if the other ranchers catch him. Or them." Morgan pushed his hat back as he turned to Seth. "You haven't missed any horses at all?"

"Not that I know about. Red here has been taking a lot of my time. Might be I should ride out tomorrow and check my herd."

"Good idea. I'll send one of my boys to go with you if you want."

"Thanks. Send Forster. He knows my horses almost as well as I do since he's worked with me before."

"Will do. I reckon I'd better head on home. We'll see you in a few days for Worth's birthday."

Seth nodded, "It'll be hard on Diane if Worth does leave."

Morgan agreed, "Hard on Laurel and me too. You wait'll Mor is grown and decides it's time to ride away on his own."

Seth's nerves tightened. It wasn't the same. Mor wasn't his flesh and blood. But he wouldn't say that to Morgan.

Suddenly Morgan laughed, "I reckon we better check in on Diane and Macee to see if they're both still alive. Diane doesn't cut Macee any slack."

Seth grinned, "Diane doesn't cut anybody any slack."

Morgan clamped a hand on Seth's shoulder. "I'm mighty glad Diane married you. You'll take good care of her and love her like she needs."

Seth managed to nod. He hoped Morgan never learned the truth about his precious daughter.

Slowly they walked to the house, Morgan once again warning Seth about the horse thief or thieves. At the door Morgan grinned at Seth, "We'll see who's out cold on the floor."

Seth chuckled, "It won't be Diane."

They stepped inside to find Diane and Macee finishing the dishes. Seth's heart jumped at seeing Diane in his kitchen again. She looked at him and he looked away quickly before she could read the love in his eyes.

"I came in to say goodbye, Diane," Morgan said.

"No!" She ran to him and threw her arms around him. He smelled like cold air and the barn. "I'll miss you, Pa."

He kissed her cheek. "And I'll miss you. You'll be over in a couple of days for Worth's birthday."

She nodded and brushed tears from her eyes. "Thanks for all you've done for me and Mor."

"Glad to help. I'm proud of that grandson of mine. First one, you know." Morgan turned to Macee. "It was nice to see you again and meet your son."

"It was good to see you too," Macee said as she dried her hands on a towel.

Barney flung his arms around Morgan's legs. "Take me with you!"

Morgan laughed and lifted Barney high in his arms. "Your momma can't get along without you. You're going home with her."

Macee pulled Barney from Morgan's arms. "He wants to go with anyone who's leaving. I think he has wanderlust in his shoes."

Barney clung to Macee. "I want to go in the sleigh."

"We're leaving soon."

"You can go now," Diane said a little too quickly. "I can manage on my own with Seth's help."

Seth curled his hat brim in his hands and didn't know what to say.

Macee turned to Seth. "I'll be back tomorrow morning to do the wash."

"Good," Seth smiled and nodded.

Diane balled the dishtowel, but didn't say anything. What good would it do to argue? For some reason Seth was determined to have Macee work for him. When he got stubborn like that, no one could budge him. But once they were alone, she'd sure try!

Morgan kissed Diane's cheek, hugged Seth, and

tipped his hat to Macee. "Diane, take good care of my grandson."

"I will, Pa." Diane held the door open for Morgan and watched him hurry to his sleigh. Cold air rushed in and she was forced to close the door. She hated to see Pa leave even though he lived only two miles away. She heard the bells jingle as he drove away. Barney pressed his nose against the windowpane and watched until he was out of sight.

Macee slipped on her coat, then held Barney's for him. "I'll be back tomorrow, Seth. Ma might be able to tend Barney so I don't have to bring him."

"Bring him. It's no bother at all." Seth ruffled Barney's hair, "No bother at all."

Diane saw the easy manner Seth used with Barney and jealousy rushed through her. Why couldn't he be that free with his own son?

Macee turned to Diane, "Goodbye, Diane."

"Goodbye," Diane said stiffly. She stood beside the table as Seth carried Barney to the sleigh with Macee walking beside him. She heard the jingle of the bells, hurried to the window, and peeked out. She watched Seth wave, then start back to the house. Her heart raced. Finally she and Seth would be alone. He started up the porch steps, hesitated, and walked back down and across the yard to the barn. Diane gasped and stepped away from the window. Was he going to the barn so he wouldn't have to be alone with her?

With a whimper she turned from the window and walked slowly to the front room. She sank down in the rocker. Fire crackled in the potbelly stove. Dust covered the small table next to the sofa and the plants sitting in front of the window on a low table. Loneliness washed over her and she suddenly wanted Mor in her arms. Maybe she should get him so she wouldn't feel so alone. But she didn't move. She looked at the piano Seth's family had left behind. Music was what this house needed!

Diane lifted the lid and sat on the bench. She softly touched the keys. The first song that popped in her head was "Billy Boy" because Barney had sung it. She played it, then laughed.

The music drifted out to Seth. A great yearning to sit in the rocker with his eyes closed and listen to Diane play rose inside him. Reluctantly he walked to the house and quietly slipped inside. He hung his coat and hat on the peg, pulled off his boots with the help of the bootjack, then silently walked to his rocker. For years he'd pictured Diane at the piano in this very room, playing for him. But in the dream they'd loved each other passionately. Tears stung his eyes, but he blinked them quickly away.

After a couple of quiet songs Diane switched to *Battle Hymn of the Republic* and played it with gusto. By the time she finished she felt much better. She turned on the bench, then gasped, "Seth! I didn't know you came in!"

"I heard you playing," he said softly.

She smiled. "I hope you liked it."

"I did."

Suddenly she realized how lonely he must have been all alone in the house. She felt bad for staying away so long. "I should've come back sooner."

He shrugged even though he wanted to tell her he'd

missed her as much as he would miss food or air if he didn't have them. "I managed. I'm sorry I didn't have the house ready for you, though."

"That's all right. It won't take me long to get it back in shape."

"With Macee's help."

Diane slowly stood, "Seth, I really don't need Macee."

"Your ma said you shouldn't lift heavy things for a while. Macee is going to come help."

"My sister could come."

"Macee needs a job."

"Oh," Diane sank back down on the bench. "Isn't there anything I can say to make you change your mind?"

"Not this time."

She frowned, "Does she really need the job or does she want to spend time with you?"

Seth stared at Diane in surprise. Was Diane jealous? What a foreign thought! "She knows I'm married."

"That doesn't bother some women."

Seth smiled suddenly, "I won't let Macee take advantage of me."

Diane's temper flared, "How can you joke about such a thing? She once loved you, you know!"

"Does that bother you?" Seth held his breath for her answer.

"Of course it bothers me! We're married! You think I want you running off with Macee Caulder and leaving me behind, a laughing-stock to the whole community?"

Seth's heart sank. He'd been wrong. Diane didn't care about him. Once again she was thinking only of herself. "I won't run away with Macee now or ever.

You should know me better than that." He gripped the arms of the rocker. "Or are you judging me by yourself?"

"What does that mean?"

"Would you run off with someone if you had the chance?"

Diane's eyes widened, "Seth! How can you even ask that?"

"No, I reckon you wouldn't. Only your heart would run off."

She trembled. Had he guessed her terrible secret - that she loved Bobby Ryder? That reminded her of what Worth had told her. She took a deep breath. "Seth, why didn't you tell me you're the one who found my diary in sixth grade?"

He stiffened. "You were all set to believe Bobby."

"You should've told me."

He shrugged, "It's over and done with."

Suddenly it came to her. He hadn't cared enough to set it straight. A great weight settled on her and she felt like she was going to cry. "I'd better check Mor."

Seth saw Diane's anguish and couldn't understand it. He watched her walk to the bedroom like a little girl who'd just had her candy snatched away. What was on her mind now? Would he ever be able to understand her?

In the bedroom Diane checked to see if Mor was still sleeping, then stood at the window and looked out at the snow. Tears blurred her eyes. Years of unhappiness stretched before her because she'd selfishly married Seth without a thought of his feeling. That night when he slept on his side of the bed as far away from her as he could get, she turned on her side and struggled against tears. If that's the way he wanted it, that's the way it would be.

The next morning Diane bathed Mor in front of the open oven door to keep him warm. She talked and cooed to him, then dressed him in soft flannel and held him to her. "I love you, Morgan Clements McGraw," she whispered. Suddenly she realized that she loved Mor just because he *was*, not for what he could do for her. It was a different love than she'd ever experienced before.

It was the same way God loved her! He loved her for herself and not for what she could do for Him!

The realization swept over her, leaving her heart leaping with joy.

Was that the way she was to love others?

The thought startled her. She'd loved Bobby because he returned her diary - not because he was Bobby. Why, she even loved Ma and Pa for what they could do for her!

"I *am* selfish just as Maureen said!" Diane's eyes filled with tears. "Forgive me, Heavenly Father. Help me to love others the way *You* do." All her life she had heard that kind of love taught. She'd seen it in action with Ma and Pa, but until now it had not been clear to her. The Holy Spirit had used her love for Mor to open her eyes to God's unselfish love.

She remembered part of a Scripture verse she'd memorized: *God's love is shed abroad in our hearts by the Holy Ghost*. Indeed, she could love like God did! It took her breath away.

Smiling, she held Mor to her as she prayed for God to show her the steps to take to practice the love that was already in her heart.

Just then the door opened and Macee walked in beside Seth who was carrying Barney. Macee looked as if she'd been crying.

Diane's muscles tightened. How she wanted to scream for Macee to take her son and leave!

Seth stood Barney on the floor. "Diane, I told Macee she and Barney could stay a while."

Diane gasped.

Macee burst into tears. "I know you don't want me, Diane, but I have no where to go. Pa told me this morning I had to get out. I don't know what's wrong with him. Ma doesn't either."

Diane thought of God's love in her heart even for Macee and she forced back her anger. She even managed to smile. "If Seth said you could stay a while, then I say so too. The house is big enough for you and Barney. You can sleep upstairs."

Seth stared at Diane in surprise. He'd expected a huge fight. He wanted to tell her he was proud of her, but the words were locked away inside him.

Macee brushed away her tears and whispered, "Thank you, Diane. I'll work hard and I'll try to stay out of the way."

"You won't be in the way," Diane said. To her surprise, she meant it.

Seth took Macee's and Barney's coats and hung them up. Was Diane going to explode the minute he was out of the room?

Diane held Mor out to Macee. "Would you like to hold Mor?"

"Oh, yes!" Macee gently took Mor and held him to

her as she sat at the table. "Barney, come see the baby. Isn't he precious?"

Barney touched Mor's head with one finger. "Is he mine?"

Macee shook her head. "He belongs to Seth and Diane."

Diane slipped her hand through Seth's arm and smiled up into his eyes.

His heart skipped a beat. What was she up to? He wanted to move away from her, but he couldn't find the strength. He liked the feel of her body against his and the smell of her clean hair.

She saw the light in his eyes before he hooded them with his lids. She thought of stepping away from him, then decided against it. If he loved her or not, she was still going to learn to let God's love shine through her for him. Maybe that's how she'd learn to love him as a wife loved a husband. She leaned her head against his arm and smiled across the room at Macee cooing to Mor.

CHAPTER 5

Excitement bubbling up inside her, Diane rode in the buggy beside Seth to Worth's birthday celebration. Enough snow had melted from the bright sun yesterday and today that they couldn't use the sleigh, but that hadn't dampened her excitement. Mor slept peacefully in her arms even over the clip-clop of horses' hooves and the rattle of the harness. She searched for something to say to get Seth into a conversation so they wouldn't have to ride in strained silence. She thought of the letter from Oregon and said, "I enjoyed the letter from your folks. I'm glad they like Oregon."

"Me too." Seth knew she was trying to get him to talk to her, but he wouldn't be drawn in.

She watched the set of his jaw. The shadow from his hat brim darkened his face. "Do you ever wish you'd gone?"

He shrugged slightly. If only she knew! "Sometimes."

Diane swallowed hard. She hadn't expected him to want to move. "Do you think you'd ever sell your place and move there?"

Seth glanced at her, then watched the horses walk quickly along the road, their ears flicking. "How could I go? You'd never be happy away from your family."

Diane's heart stopped. Seth was putting her above his desire to go to Oregon! What did that mean? She couldn't sort it out right now, but she'd think about it later. She finally said, "If you want to move to Oregon, I'll go with you."

Seth tightened his hold on the reins. What game was she playing now? "Don't say something you don't mean," he said hoarsely.

"But I do mean it!"

"Why? To get away from...someone?" He was going to say Bobby, but he couldn't say the name aloud.

"You mean Macee? No, I don't want to get away from her." Diane laughed. "You might not believe this, but we haven't argued since she's been with us."

He had noticed, but he thought they kept the peace only when he was around. "I'm glad to hear that."

Diane frowned in thought as she looked up at the bright sky without noticing the fluffy white clouds. "I wonder why her pa made her leave. It's strange, isn't it?"

"I never thought about it."

"I have. I know Jack Cannon. He dotes on her!" Diane tapped Seth's arm. "Just like you will when we have a daughter."

Seth's pulse leaped, then turned to ice. He'd thought he could forgive and forget what Diane had done, but so far he hadn't been able to touch her or kiss her. He kept busy with daily chores, training Red Lightning, and checking the horses in the winter pasture to see if they were all there. Forster had ridden out twice with him and they found all the horses. Each night he was too bone weary to do anything but fall into bed and sleep soundly. He never heard Mor in the night even though Diane said he cried.

Diane peeked at Seth through her lashes. What was he thinking to make him so upset? Was he determined they wouldn't have another baby? Could he love all babies but his own? She looked down at Mor all bundled in warm blankets. What would Mor do if Seth rejected him later as he was now? A great sadness rose inside Diane for Mor and even for Seth for what he was missing by ignoring his baby. Silently she prayed for Seth. She didn't speak again about having another baby.

She looked up just in time to see Bobby Ryder riding his black horse around a snowy hill. She sucked in her breath. Why was Bobby on Pa's property again? Was he the horse thief? She forced the terrible thought away faster than it had flicked through her mind. Bobby would never steal someone's horse! He knew good and well that a horse thief was the lowest criminal alive. And he knew it meant death by hanging. Diane shook her head. No, Bobby would never steal a horse.

Then why was he where he didn't belong?

Diane stiffened. Was Bobby going to visit Macee? A band squeezed Diane's heart until she almost cried out in agony. Tears burned her eyes. Then she remembered the truth about Bobby. He had never loved her. Her feelings for him hadn't been real love. She was saving her real love for Seth.

Impatiently she pushed aside thoughts of Bobby. She would ask Macee if Bobby came to call while they were away. If not, she'd find a way to learn why he was trespassing again.

Seth glanced at Diane. He knew he'd hurt her by not responding when she said he'd dote on their daughter. He wanted to make amends before they reached Morgan's ranch. He searched around for something to say and settled on talking about Worth. "Will you be okay about Worth leaving?"

"Yes," she said in a tiny voice. She'd asked God for special strength to let Worth lead the life he chose, not the life she wanted for him. That was true love. Oh, but it was hard!

"Good. I talked to him about it and he's excited about going."

"Do you wish you could do the same thing?"

"I reckon. Sometimes anyway."

Diane frowned, "But why? I'm satisfied staying here. Why can't the rest of the family be?"

"They're all different. You can't have cookie-cutter people."

Diane giggled. "That's good, Seth. Cookie-cutter people." Then she sobered. "I suppose that's what I want. I'll try not to."

Seth studied Diane in surprise. She'd been surprising him a lot in the last two days. What had happened to make her different? He didn't ask her in case it had something to do with Bobby.

At the ranch Butch ran to meet them, barking and waving his tail. Smoke curled up from the chimney into the bright blue sky. Butch leaped high as if he'd jump into the buggy.

Diane laughed. "Stop it, Butch!"

He stopped barking and ran beside the buggy until Seth drew up near the porch for Diane to alight.

The door burst open, letting out the sounds of singing around the piano. Worth ran out without his jacket or hat. He wore a red plaid shirt and levis that fit snug against his lean frame. "Diane! Seth! I'm glad to see you!"

"Happy birthday, Worth!" Diane and Seth said together.

"Thank you." Worth's eyes sparkled and he looked happier than he had in a long time.

Diane's stomach lurched. Was Worth that happy to get away? She handed Mor to Worth, then climbed to the ground. Slowly she walked up the steps beside Worth as Seth drove the buggy to the barn. "You're really leaving, aren't you, Worth?"

He nodded. "Be happy for me, Di. What you think means a lot to me."

Diane hugged Worth, careful not to squeeze Mor in Worth's arm. "I will be happy because it's what you want." She told him what God had taught her about love. "So, that's why I can send you off without bursting into wild tears."

Worth kissed Diane's pink cheek. "I love you, big sister."

"And I love you! Really love you!"

Worth nodded. "You're special, Diane. I promise I'll write. And I promise I won't stay away forever."

"Thank you."

His eyes twinkled. "Only long enough to find a greenhorn wife."

Diane jabbed Worth's arm. "Let's get inside so I can

unwrap Mor."

"You take Mor. I want to talk to Seth while we can have a minute of silence. You sure won't find silence inside the house." Chuckling, Worth laid Mor in Diane's arms, then ran to meet Seth on his way across the yard. Diane watched them greet each other. They were the same build and dressed almost alike. Seth's red hair was bright next to Worth's blonde. Diane's heart swelled with pride. The two men were very important to her.

Smiling, she walked into the house. No one heard her and she breathed in the smell that was home - or once had been home. Worth's birthday cake covered with twenty-four candles sat in the middle of the oval table. The cake was chocolate with chocolate frosting - the kind he wanted every year. Where would he be for his next birthday?

Diane bit her lip and turned away from the cake. She eased out of her coat and hung it over Pa's, then peeled back Mor's blankets. Oh, he looked beautiful all snug and warm and fast asleep. His mouth looked like Seth's. Had he even noticed? But how could he? He wouldn't look at Mor even when he held him. After Ma had put Mor in Seth's arms that day she thought everything would be fine, but it wasn't. Seth would hold Mor once in a while, but never again had he looked at him or nuzzled his cheeks or smiled at him. Something was very wrong. "What can it be?" Diane whispered as she draped the extra blankets over the back of the chair. Maybe she should ask him. Would he tell her?

Just then Laurel walked into the kitchen. With a glad cry she hugged Diane, then took Mor. "How's my precious grandson today? You're so beautiful, sweetheart."

Diane beamed with pride.

"I believe his hair is getting a red cast to it," Laurel said in surprise as she held Mor out to get a better look. "It is! Look, Di!"

She laughed. "I think you're right. His hair is auburn like Garrett's." Diane touched her curly blonde fringe. "Do you think it'll ever turn blonde like mine?"

"It could. I've seen dark-headed babies turn tow-headed." Smiling proudly, Laurel held Mor tight to her. "The others will want to see him. And you too, Diane."

Diane chuckled. "Be sure to add that, Ma. Don't think I don't realize Mor will get more attention than I will." She followed Ma to the front room where the singing was louder.

Outdoors Worth and Seth stopped on the porch and stood side by side looking off across the prairie. Slapping his tail against the porch floor, Butch lay at Worth's feet.

"I'll miss you," Worth said without looking at Seth.

"And I you. I love you like I do my own brothers."

Worth grinned and jabbed Seth's arm. "I'll be back. I promised Diane I wouldn't stay away forever. And I mean it. But I gotta see what's out there!"

"I understand, Worth. I'm glad you're able to go."

"Tomorrow I'll take the stage south to the railroad, then the train all the way to Chambers, New York, where Grandpa came from. He was seven years-old when they made the trip west in a covered wagon." Worth laughed softly. "Think of that, Seth! They left what they knew to come to a wilderness!"

"Sometimes I wonder if I'd have the courage to do

that."

"Me too." Worth crossed his arms to warm himself. "It took me a while to get the courage to go back east. But I'm finally going!"

A lump lodged in Seth's throat and he couldn't speak for a while. "God is with you even as you go east."

"I know."

"We'll be praying for you."

"Thanks. And I'll be praying for you and Diane. I know something's wrong between the two of you."

Seth backed away, his face closed.

"Don't worry. I'm not going to ask you about it. Just remember, I'll be praying as I have been all along."

"Thank you. I appreciate it." Tears smarted Seth's eyes. "I sure do love you, Worth."

Worth wrapped his arms around Seth and slapped his back. He pulled away and jabbed Seth in the arm. "I didn't mean to get all mushy - as Maureen says."

"I don't mind a bit." Seth laughed. "This is some family. I sure am proud to belong to it."

Worth chuckled, "Me too." He took a deep breath and ran his fingers through his short blonde hair. "I'll miss them. But I have to go, Seth. I don't know why, but I know I must."

"You'll have a great time. Be sure to write. Diane will need to hear from you."

"She's taking my leaving a lot better than I thought she would." Worth told Seth what Diane had said.

Seth listened in surprise. So, that's why he'd seen a change in Diane. Was it possible for her to put Bobby out of her heart to make room for.... Seth wouldn't let himself finish the thought. "Let's go inside before you freeze."

"Or before somebody decides to eat my cake without me," Worth said with a laugh.

Later, after dinner and the chocolate birthday cake had been served, Diane gently laid Mor in Alane's basket. She dressed for outdoors and ran out to join the snowball fight Forster had planned. He'd built a fort for both teams, but the sun had partly melted them already. Laughter rang across the yard as everyone teased back and forth on who was going to win the snowball battle. Barking wildly, Butch ran from one person to another.

Diane picked up a handful of wet snow and formed it into a ball as she ran to Forster's side.

"I'm ready," Diane said just as a snowball struck her in the leg. She barely felt it through her wool skirt and two petticoats, but she spun around to find the guilty party. "Who did that? The game hasn't started yet."

"It was Seth!" Alane cried, even though she'd thrown it.

Diane giggled and threw her snowball at Seth. He dodged and the snowball landed near the chicken coop. "I'll get you next time, Seth McGraw!"

His heart jerked as he heard the laughter in Diane's voice and saw her sparkling eyes and rosy red cheeks. Was he falling deeper in love with her? He dare not or he couldn't survive what she'd done. He turned away without saying anything to her.

She shrugged and ran behind the fort with Forster and Maureen. The others were on Garrett's team across the yard behind the half-melted fort. "Hey, it's not fair!

You have four and we have three," Diane called.

"We have Alane," Garrett shouted, "and we all know what a poor aim she has."

"Can't aim, huh?" Alane threw a snowball at Garrett and hit him, then bent over laughing. She'd hit him because he was standing so close, but she had a poor aim if she was too far from her target.

Diane picked up a snowball from the pile Forster had made so they wouldn't run out.

Forster lifted his hand high in the sky. "Let the battle begin!"

Snowballs flew through the air, some falling short and others hitting their targets. Diane felt as if she was in school again. She took careful aim and hit Seth in the leg, then laughed and jumped up and down with glee.

Seth laughed and hit her in the shoulder with a snowball. It felt good to put his agony aside and play again. By the time the game was over, even his long underwear was wet and he was beginning to feel the cold.

"We won!" Alane shouted, jumping with joy.

"We did!" Maureen cried, her face red and her nutmeg-brown hair wet.

"It's a tie," Forster said with a laugh.

As the others ran toward the house laughing and talking, Seth bent down to get his hat from a snowdrift where it had fallen earlier in the game.

Unexpectedly Diane flung herself at him and knocked him back into the snowdrift. "I got you now," she said with a laugh as she fell on top of him, a snowball in her hand. She started to rub it in his face, but he caught her wrist and held her hand away from his face. With a laugh she lowered her head and kissed him fully on the lips. They were cold and firm.

A flame sprang up inside him and he fiercely caught her to him. He kissed her as if he'd never let her go.

She tried to pull away, but couldn't. She felt dizzy and weak, then gave herself up to his kisses. He'd never kissed her with such abandonment. The more he kissed her, the more she wanted. Never in her life had she felt such a rush of emotion.

Suddenly Seth pushed her away and sat up, his breathing ragged and his face red. Had the others seen him get so carried away? "I'm sorry," he muttered.

Diane laughed shakily. She'd never dreamed Seth could be so passionate. "Sorry for what? I am your wife."

He looked around, but no one was in sight. "I reckon they all went inside."

Her eyes twinkling, Diane scooped up Seth's hat and jumped to her feet. She held his hat high. "Is this what you were after?"

He leaped up but before he could get his hat, she ran off like a shot. The girl he'd loved in school was back, but now she was an adult. She was his wife. Love for her blazed so high he felt weak all over.

Diane jumped up on the porch and waved his hat in the air. "Come and get it, Seth. What's the matter? Getting old?" She giggled and waved his hat again.

Laughing, he ran to the porch. "I'll never get old!"

She held his hat behind her back. "Give me a kiss and I'll give you your hat."

He saw the brilliant blue of her eyes as he bent to kiss her, then before his lips touched hers, he grabbed his hat. It took all his will power to laugh and walk inside without kissing her.

She hesitated, her finger on her lips where she could still feel his kisses. Why couldn't he always be passionate instead of guarded and restrained? Maybe it had been her fault. She'd always been guarded and restrained with him. Today was the first time since they were married that she initiated a kiss. She giggled. Maybe she'd just have to do it more often.

Seth stuck his head out the door. Once again his eyes were cold as he looked at her. "Your baby's crying."

Diane frowned. *Your* baby? "Get him, would you? I'll be right in."

Seth closed the door with a sharp bang.

Diane bit her lip and tried to sort out what had happened. Was Seth upset because she'd kissed him or because the baby was crying and she wasn't right there to tend him? And why did Seth call Mor *her* baby, not *their* baby? A great sadness filled her and she sagged against the porch. Why couldn't her life be full of happiness all the time?

The door opened and Worth stepped out, dressed in dry clothes. "Is something wrong, Di?"

She nodded. "But I don't know what it is," she whispered.

He wrapped his arms around her and held her close.

She clung to him and pressed her face into his strong shoulder. "Please don't leave me, Worth. I need you too much!"

He sighed and tipped up her face. "God is with you, Diane. Think about what you told me a while ago - God's love is shed abroad in your heart. The other side of that love is God loves you so much He wants the very best for you. He yearns to help you with your problems. He is the answer for them!"

Worth's words soaked deeply into her and she nodded. God did want the very best for her! He did want to help her find answers to her problems! Even to Seth's strange behavior. Silently she prayed she would understand Seth's conduct so she could deal with it. She smiled mistily at Worth, "Thank you."

"What're brothers for?" He kissed her cheek. "That's my goodbye. I know you'll be leaving soon and the family will mob you, but I wanted a minute alone with you." He rubbed a tear off her cold cheek. "Thanks for letting me go without throwing a fit."

She giggled. "Now would I do that?"

"Yes. But no longer. I'm happy to see the change."

She nodded.

"Di, something's eating away at Seth. Find out what it is and help him deal with it."

"I plan to."

"Good. Write to me, will you?"

"Of course!" She hugged him tightly. "You be careful, you hear me, Worth Clements?"

"I hear you, you little mother you."

She laughed shakily.

"I love you, Diane." He lifted her face and looked deeply into her eyes. "Thank you for all the years of mothering and love."

"Please don't say that! It sounds so...so final!"

"It's not. I'll be back. I promise!"

"And I'll hold you to that promise!"

He held her close a minute longer, then pushed her toward the door. "I shouldn't have kept you so long.

Mor is crying for you."

"Was Seth holding him?"

"No. Ma."

Diane brushed away signs of tears and hurried inside to Mor.

Later Diane rode in the buggy beside Seth. She was tired and Mor was cranky from being held so much. Seth was quiet, as usual. Diane jiggled Mor to get him to stop crying, but nothing worked. Finally she turned impatiently to Seth. "Please hold him a while. I'll drive."

Seth hesitated, then switched with her. He felt awkward holding Mor with all his blankets. "Maybe he's too warm."

"I don't think so." Diane flicked the reins to get the horses to move faster. The sooner they got home, the sooner she could get Mor in his cradle. She wanted to talk about the wonderful day, but couldn't over Mor's crying. She was even too exhausted to relive Seth's kisses.

Seth held Mor tightly to him as Laurel had taught him to do. Finally Mor stopped crying.

Diane smiled at Seth. "A father's touch. That's all it took."

"Watch where you're driving!" Seth saw the pain flash in Diane's eyes at his sharp words, but he didn't take them back. He was not Mor's father! He flushed with guilt. Somehow he had to come to grips with his anguish. Why did he keep taking it back after he'd given it to the Lord?

Several minutes later Diane stopped the buggy beside

the porch and climbed out. She took Mor from Seth and hurried inside without a word to Seth. Right now she couldn't deal with his anger.

She stopped just inside the kitchen. The house was quiet but warm. She shrugged out of her coat and took off her wet boots, then hurried to her bedroom. Where were Macee and Barney? It was too early for them to be in bed.

Pushing the thoughts aside, Diane unwrapped Mor and carefully laid him in his cradle. He moaned and rubbed his cheek against the sheet without waking up. She covered him and walked quietly from the room. In relief she sank down in her rocker and leaned her head back. "Blessed silence," she whispered with her eyes closed.

As she sat there an uneasiness spread through her. Something was wrong. She pushed herself up. Maybe she should check to see if Macee was asleep upstairs.

Holding the bannister Diane walked silently up the wooden steps and peeked in the bedroom Macee was using. A bright quilt was spread neatly over the bed. Macee's clothes hung on pegs, but Macee wasn't there. Diane looked across the hall in the room Barney used. It was empty too, but just as tidy. "Maybe she went to visit her family," Diane muttered as she walked downstairs.

She fixed the fire in the front room and the kitchen, then put the teakettle on to boil. Suddenly she gasped. What if Macee was with Bobby Ryder?

Diane lifted her chin and said firmly, "If she is, she is! I don't care!"

Just then a paper under the table caught her attention. She bent and picked it up. It was a note from Macee saying they'd driven to town, but would be back before dark. "That solves that mystery," Diane muttered with a grin.

She looked out the window. It would be dark soon. She tried to see Seth, but couldn't. He was probably in the barn.

Outdoors Seth stood in back of the corral after turning the team loose and looked toward the pasture with a frown. He saw the bull standing near a dark blob in the grass. What was it? Had a piece of clothing blown into the pasture? "I'd best check," he said crisply.

He stepped inside the barn, lifted down the bullwhip, and hung it over his shoulder. He didn't trust the bull any further than he could throw him.

As Seth drew closer to the pasture his breath caught in his throat. The blob looked like a person. But that couldn't be. He climbed through the fence and walked closer still. The bull roared and pawed the ground. Steam rose from his nose.

"Get!" Seth shouted. The bull bellowed and started toward Seth. He cracked his whip and the noise rang across the prairie. "I said get!" The bull ran away awkwardly and stopped near the naked cottonwood tree several yards away.

His nerves stretched tight, Seth finally reached the object. It was a man! With a gasp Seth peered closer. His blood ran cold. It was Bobby Ryder!

His heart racing, Seth jumped back. Let the bull have Bobby!

Bobby moaned.

His mouth bone dry, Seth bent back over Bobby. Blood and dirt covered his face and jacket. The bull had gored and trampled him! If he stayed where he was, he'd freeze to death during the night.

"Let him," Seth muttered angrily. He started to walk away, then stopped. What was he thinking? He couldn't leave anyone, not even Bobby Ryder, to die. Seth closed his eyes and gripped the whip tightly. If he took Bobby inside, Diane would fall all over him with love and concern. He looked too badly hurt to drive him to the doc.

Seth rubbed a gloved hand across his face. If he took Bobby to his house, could he handle seeing Diane's love for Bobby?

Seth thought of Diane's kisses today and the way she'd teased him. He wanted her to be that way always! But would she remember he even existed if he carried Bobby inside for her to nurse back to health?

Deep inside he heard God gently say, "Take care of Bobby."

Seth recoiled under the weight of the great task set before him. Could he survive seeing Bobby in his house with his wife?

Shaking his head, he said, "It doesn't matter. I must take him in. God, please help me."

Carefully Seth eased Bobby over his shoulder and lifted him. He staggered under Bobby's weight, then slowly walked toward the fence.

CHAPTER 6

His stomach a hard knot, Seth eased the door open and stepped into the warm kitchen with Bobby over his shoulder.

"Seth!" Her blonde hair loose and flowing about her shoulders, Diane rushed to him. "Who's that? What's wrong? You have blood on you! Are you hurt?"

"I'm fine."

Shivers ran down her spine as she followed Seth across the kitchen and looked closer at the body he carried. "Bobby Ryder!" Her legs almost collapsed, but she stiffened them to follow Seth across the front room. "Oh, Seth! Is he...dead?"

"No. But hurt bad." Blocking out the anguish he heard in Diane's voice, Seth carried Bobby up the stairs with Diane running after him. In the hallway, she ducked around Seth and hurried into the unused bedroom. She pulled back the covers and stepped aside as Seth laid Bobby down.

Bobby moaned.

"He looks awful! What on earth happened to him and where'd you find him?" Diane bent over Bobby to check the wounds on his face. It was hard to see through all the blood and dirt.

Seth explained about finding Bobby as he watched her and saw the concern on her face. Seth's heart twisted painfully. How he wished God had not told him to help Bobby!

Diane turned wide eyes on Seth. "Will he be all right?"

"I'll undress him." Seth eased Diane aside and pulled off Bobby's jacket and boots, then his shirt and levis. "He's soaked through. Turn around while I take off his longjohns."

Diane obediently turned around. "I wonder why he was in our pasture?"

Seth didn't want to consider the answer right then as he carefully pulled off the longjohns. Bobby's dark skin was covered with bruises, but the only broken skin was on his face. Maybe the bull hadn't gored him. Seth covered Bobby with the sheet and blanket, then stepped away from the bed with Bobby's clothes in a bundle in his arms. "I'll take these to the back room."

"Good. Hang them over the rack to dry." Diane hurried to Macee's room and brought back the pitcher and bowl of water.

Seth moved restlessly, "I'll get doc and be back as soon as I can."

Diane turned pain-filled eyes to him. "Be careful, Seth. It'll be dark soon."

"I'll be all right." He couldn't help but add, "Will you be?"

"Yes. Macee should be back any minute, then she'll help me."

Seth stood stock still. Diane was going to allow Macee to help with Bobby! Was Diane's love for Bobby fading?

Diane gently wiped the blood from Bobby's face. "You'll be all right, Bobby. I'm here."

Seth heard the tender concern in Diane's voice and his heart sank. Slowly he walked downstairs to the back room and draped Bobby's clothes over the rack near the neatly stacked wood pile.

In the kitchen Seth pulled open the door to step outdoors just as Macee and Barney started across the porch.

"What's wrong?" Macee asked sharply at seeing Seth's face.

"Bobby Ryder's hurt bad upstairs."

"Bobby?" Macee slumped in a faint and Seth leaped forward and caught her before she hit the porch floor. He easily carried her inside and set her on a kitchen chair. Sobbing hard, Barney followed them.

"Ma," he said, tugging on her coat sleeve.

"She'll be all right," Seth said gently. He couldn't understand why she'd fainted. He took off her bonnet and coat. Loose strands of her strawberry-blonde hair clung to her cheeks.

She revived almost immediately and tried to stand, but Seth held her down with a firm hand on her shoulder.

Barney stopped crying and rubbed his eyes with his fists.

Seth patted Macee's shoulder. "Relax a minute so you don't faint again."

She pressed her trembling hands to her heart. "I have

to see Bobby!"

"Me too!" Barney cried as he dropped his coat and hat on the floor.

"Diane's with him."

"Did he get shot?" Macee rung her hands and started to cry. "I told him it might happen!"

Seth frowned questioningly at her. Why would she think he got shot? "He didn't get shot. My bull trampled him."

Macee gasped, "No!"

"In the pasture on the other side of the corral."

Macee knocked away Seth's hand and jumped up. "He must've been out there a long time!"

"I couldn't tell. I'm going after doc now."

Trembling, Macee pushed past Seth and said over her shoulder, "Doc's with Mrs. Treebel north of town. She's having her baby and he said he'd be there until tomorrow sometime."

Seth groaned.

"I can take care of Bobby!" She ran for the stairs with Barney on her heels.

Helplessly Seth shook his head. Was Macee in love with Bobby too? What did the man have that women flocked to him? It sure wasn't honesty and integrity!

His ears tuned to sounds from upstairs, Seth fixed the fires, picked up the milk pail and the egg basket and headed out to do the chores. If he kept busy, he wouldn't have time to think about Diane touching Bobby and crying over him.

Upstairs Diane reluctantly moved aside to make room for Macee. She carefully checked to see if Bobby had any broken ribs while Barney stood on the trunk and leaned over the footboard to watch.

Macee sighed in relief. "None broken, but his ribs are bruised and he'll hurt a long time." Macee brushed away a tear. "I'll have to sew up the cut on his cheek."

Diane gasped, "Can you do that?"

Macee nodded, "I've done it many times." She laughed dryly. "I even considered being a doctor at one time, then decided it was too hard. I've read that the few women doctors there are are scorned by everyone - even other women."

"It would seem strange to have a woman doctor," Diane locked her icy hands together. Talking about women doctors was the furthest thing from her mind. She wanted to talk about Bobby and why he'd been in the pasture and what Macee knew about it. The words stuck on Diane's tongue. She knew Macee was too upset to answer those questions.

His face white, Barney leaned over the footboard and looked at Bobby. "Is he gonna die like Pa did?"

Macee snatched Barney up in her arms and held him fiercely. "No! He's not going to die. He's not hurt bad like Pa was. We'll work together to make him better."

Bobby groaned and opened his eyes, "Macee?"

She put Barney down, then fell on her knees beside the bed and took Bobby's hand. "You're going to be all right."

Diane bit her lip. She wanted to be the one Bobby spoke to first, but he didn't even notice her.

"I couldn't get the horse."

"Shhh!" Macee covered his mouth with her fingertips, then looked quickly back at Diane. "When he stopped by, his horse ran off through the pasture and he went after it. I thought he was already gone when me and Barney went to town."

The story didn't set right with Diane, but she let it pass. She moved enough so Bobby could see her. "We'll take care of you, Bobby. Macee and I will."

Bobby moved, then gasped from the pain. "I hurt all over."

Macee touched his face. "You have a cut on your cheek I must sew up. It'll hurt. Can you stand it?"

"I reckon I'll have to." Bobby smiled at Barney. "Partner, you run on out of here so you don't see me cry."

Macee smiled at her son. "Go to your room until I finish working on Bobby. I'll call you when I'm done."

Barney lifted his chin and looked determined. "I want to stay."

"No!" Macee walked Barney to the door. "Stay in your room like I said. I mean it!"

"Yes, Ma." Sighing, Barney walked to his room.

"I'll get my needle and thread," Macee said over her should to Diane. "Don't let him move around."

"I won't." When Macee left the room, Diane knelt beside the bed and took Bobby's hand. "I feel terrible about what our bull did to you."

"Not as terrible as me," Bobby squeezed her hand and groaned at the pain that shot through him. "How'd I get in here?"

"Seth carried you."

Bobby's eyes widened, "You don't say!"

"It shouldn't surprise you. Seth's a fine man."

Groaning, Bobby closed his eyes. How could Seth do anything for him after what Bobby had done to him? "I want out of here," Bobby muttered.

"You're too banged up to be moved and doc is busy delivering a baby."

Bobby's eyes flashed. He would not stay in Seth's house! "You help me up and let me go!"

"No! If you're going to talk, talk about something else. You are not leaving until you're well enough!"

Bobby sighed and didn't argue further. He glanced at Diane again. "I hear you had a boy."

"Yes," Diane smiled proudly. "Morgan Clements McGraw. We call him Mor."

"Red hair?"

"Dark."

Bobby groaned. Seth was sure to think the worst. Yet, he'd brought him into his own home to nurse him back to health! What kind of man was he?

"What's wrong?" Diane asked sharply at the anguish she saw on Bobby's face.

He couldn't speak for a while, then finally whispered, "Nothing."

Diane let it go. She didn't want him agitated more than he already was.

Macee hurried into the room with the needle and thread. "I had to hunt for the right thread."

Diane reluctantly stood aside again. It was hard to imagine squeamish Macee could actually tend an injured man. "Tell me how I can help."

"Hold his head still." Macee bent over Bobby and looked him right in the eye. "Bobby, you're going to have to be as quiet as possible."

"I need a bullet to bite on."

Macee managed to laugh, "Sorry, I don't have one."

Bobby glanced around, then remembered he'd left his gun and holster hooked over his saddle horn. When they were alone, he'd tell Macee that Spade was tied to a tree out of sight of the ranch buildings. Macee would have to get Spade before Seth found him and really got suspicious. But how could she get him with the bull loose in the pasture? It was too much to think about when he was hurting so badly.

Macee patted Bobby's shoulder. "Relax, Bobby. It won't take me long."

Diane trembled and thought she was going to faint. She couldn't stand seeing Macee sew Bobby's cheek.

Macee lit a match and held the needle over it to sterilize it. Could she keep her hand steady while she sewed up Bobby? She had no choice. She showed Diane where to hold Bobby, then she carefully pricked his skin with the needle. He flinched, but didn't cry out. She took five stitches before she was finished. Sweat soaked Bobby's face and her's too.

Feeling light-headed, Diane turned away and gulped great gulps of air. She saw Barney standing in the doorway, his face white and his eyes large.

"Did he die?" Barney asked.

Diane shook her head.

Macee hurried to Barney and lifted him in her arms. "Come see for yourself." She carried him to the side of the bed. "See! He's fine. But his cheek looks like a stitched patch on your pants."

Barney laughed and squirmed to get down. He leaned against the bed near Bobby's arm. "You okay, Bobby?"

Bobby smiled crookedly, "Sure am. But I think I'm

going to sleep right now. I feel woozy."

Diane did too, but she also felt in the way. Silently she walked away. She gripped the bannister for support as she crept downstairs. She checked on Mor to make sure he was sleeping soundly, then hurried to the rocker in the front room and collapsed in it. She shivered, then shivered again. Bobby was upstairs in pain and she couldn't be with him! She frowned. But isn't that what she'd decided? It was wrong for her to care about Bobby the way she had the past several years. It was especially wrong when she wanted to learn to love Seth. She frowned. No, it was wrong because she was *married* to Seth! How could God's love be shed abroad in her heart if she continued to sin by loving another man? She must stop loving Bobby. She groaned. Oh, it was so easy to say, and so hard to do!

Diane glanced at the table beside her that held the worn Bible she'd been reading since she was a little girl. With God's help she could obey. She'd known that when she was a child but, for some reason, had forgotten it lately.

Could she handle having Bobby upstairs with Macee fawning over him?

Before she could answer her own question, Mor cried and she hurried to him. She lit the lamp on the dresser, changed Mor's diaper, then sat down to nurse him. The murmur of voices drifted downstairs. Her jaw tightened. Bobby had come to see Macee today! Why had he turned his horse into the pasture? It didn't make sense. Maybe she should talk to Maureen about it. Maureen loved solving mysteries.

Forcing away thoughts of Bobby and Macee so she

could enjoy time with her baby, Diane held Mor to her shoulder and burped him. Smiling, she rubbed her cheek against his soft hair. Seth had no idea what he was missing by ignoring Mor.

Now, that was another mystery. But she dare not talk to Maureen about that. It was too private and personal.

She heard the kitchen door open and Seth walk in. With Mor at her shoulder she hurried to the kitchen. Seth was just lighting the lamp. The smell of sulfur wafted through the room, then was gone.

Seth shook out the match and put the globe in place. He turned the wick down to keep the flame from blackening the globe, then looked up at Diane. His heart jerked at the picture she and Mor made. If only Mor were his! "How's Bobby?"

"Fine. Macee checked him over for broken bones. He didn't have any. Then she sewed the cut in his cheek. She's still up there with him."

"Why aren't you?"

She shrugged, "I felt out of place."

"Oh?"

She didn't want to go into it, so she asked, "Did you find Bobby's horse, Spade?"

"No."

"He rode Spade here and turned him into the pasture, or so Bobby said. Would Spade go back to Nick Stone's place?"

"He couldn't get out of the pasture without jumping the fence. I'll ask Bobby about him."

"It'll have to wait until tomorrow with the way Macee's watching over him." Diane sat at the table and watched Seth strain the milk, then rinse the bucket with boiling water. A basket of eggs that he'd gathered sat on the table. "How's Red Lightning?" Diane held her breath for Seth's answer. Was she expecting him to say Red was gone?

"He's feisty tonight. Like a storm's coming."

Diane breathed a sigh of relief, then said, "I hope it doesn't snow again, especially for Worth's trip."

"The stage always makes it through."

"I know. I want everything to be nice for Worth."

Seth's face softened, "He'll be all right, Di."

"I know," she whispered.

He wanted to hold her close. Before he gave in to it, he turned away to set the bucket upside down to dry for the morning.

Barney ran into the room and flung himself at Seth. "I'm hungry, Seth! Can you feed me?"

Laughing, Seth lifted Barney up. "I know your momma baked bread today. Want a bowl of bread and milk?"

"Sure."

Diane watched Seth and Barney together while Seth broke a slice of bread into pieces in a bowl. He poured milk over it, set it in front of Barney and handed him a spoon from the fancy glass spoon jar in the center of the table.

Seth felt Diane's eyes on him and he glanced at her. She had a look of yearning on her face that made his heart turn over. What was she thinking? How could he bring back the sparkle her eyes had during the snowball fight?

Just then Macee walked in, her face pale. "He's finally asleep." She sank to a chair with a long sigh.

"Did he die?" Barney asked, his spoon suspended between his mouth and bowl. Milk dripped off the spoon.

"No, Barney. He's alive and he's going to stay alive." Macee smiled at Barney. "When you're done eating, we'll go back upstairs and you can see for yourself."

Seth pushed three pieces of wood into the stove and closed the lid. He wanted to talk to Macee about Bobby, but not in front of Barney. "Macee, could you come down a while after you tuck Barney into bed so we can talk?"

Macee tensed, then nodded. She'd have to be very careful what she said to Seth or they'd be out in the cold yet tonight.

Diane saw Macee's tension and wondered about it. Hopefully Seth would let her stay in the kitchen when he talked to Macee.

The teakettle boiled, sending spatters of water dancing across the cast iron top of the stove. Seth made himself a cup of tea and asked Macee and Diane if they wanted one. They both declined.

Diane moved restlessly as Macee and Seth talked about old times at school. Finally Macee excused herself and Barney and walked upstairs.

Her jaw set with determination, Diane jumped up and stepped around the table where Seth was sitting. She'd get him to hold Mor if it was the last thing she did! "Hold Mor a while, would you, please?"

Seth frowned. He couldn't do it, not with Bobby upstairs. "He's asleep. Put him in his cradle."

Diane's anger snapped. "How can you hold Barney

and play with him, and not Mor?"

"I don't want to get into a fight tonight," Seth said tiredly.

"I don't understand why you don't even like our baby." Tears welled up in Diane's eyes, clung to her lashes, then rolled down her pale cheeks. "You're his father. Can't you act like it?"

Seth's blood ran cold. How could Diane say that when Mor's real father lay upstairs? "I don't want to fight with you tonight," he said hoarsely.

"What will you be saying to Mor when he's three? How will he feel when you won't play with him or talk to him like you do Barney?"

So that's what was bothering her! Seth scraped back his chair and stood. "I'll put him to bed for you. Fix yourself a cup of tea and calm down."

His words sent a fresh burst of anger through Diane. She wanted to scream at him, but she couldn't or it would wake Mor and frighten the others. She held Mor out to Seth, then grabbed her coat. "I'm going out for a walk."

Seth bit back a sharp answer as he gingerly carried Mor to his cradle. Seth laid Mor on his stomach and covered him up. What would he do when Mor was older? Somehow he had to get his feelings under control so he could learn to love Mor.

Outdoors Diane breathed in the crisp, cold air as she carefully walked across the yard. It was icy in spots, dry in other places, and snowy where the sun hadn't reached today. The moon was bright enough to cast shadows. This was a night for people in love, not a husband and wife who practically hated each other. She frowned. "I don't hate Seth," she said sharply.

A horse in the corral nickered. In the distance an owl hooted. Snow crunched under her feet as she walked to the closed barn door. She had a sudden urge to check Red Lightning.

Inside the barn she struck a match and lit the lantern that always hung on a hook just inside the door. She smelled the sulfur and kerosene along with the pungent odor of the barn. The wood creaked and mice scurried across the haymow. She walked along the hard-packed dirt aisle to Red's stall. Stalls lined both sides of the wide aisle. She lifted the lantern, then cried out. The stall was empty! She lifted the lantern higher to check each corner of the small stall. It was indeed empty. She ran to the barn door, hung the lantern on the hook, then raced to the house. She burst into the kitchen, her hair wild and her eyes wide with fright. "Seth, come quick! Red's gone!"

"No!" Seth grabbed his coat and slipped it on as he ran to the barn with her. Morgan had been right about a horse thief!

In the barn Seth grabbed the lantern and ran to a stall at the back of the barn.

"Where're you going?" Diane cried, stopping at Red's stall.

"Down here. I moved Red this evening since I didn't have time to clean his stall."

Diane's face flamed, "I didn't know."

Seth held the lantern high just as Red nickered. Seth turned back to Diane. "Why'd you tell me she was gone?"

"I thought she was. I'm sorry. I feel so foolish!" Slowly Diane walked toward Seth. "I didn't think to check another stall. I was scared and thought Pa was right."

Seth grinned, "I'm sure glad you were wrong."

"Me too!" Diane patted Red's face. "You're a real beauty, Red. If anybody tries to take you, you scream and kick."

Seth hung the lantern on a nearby hook and leaned against the stall door beside Diane. "I'll keep close watch on Red after what your pa said."

"Good," Diane moved close to Seth and slipped her hand through his arm. She felt him stiffen, but she didn't pull away. "How soon will the buyer be here for Red?"

"Sometime next month." Seth could barely think with Diane so close to him.

"I'll be glad when I can help train horses again."

"How can you with the baby?"

Diane shrugged, "When he's asleep." She smiled into his eyes. "It's nice being out here - just the two of us," she said softly.

Why was she doing this to him? He wasn't made of iron, after all. "We'd better get back inside."

"Mor's asleep and Macee will wait for us." Diane inched between the stall and Seth, then slipped her arms around his neck. "Do you know Pa still kisses Ma every chance he gets? Will we be doing that after we're married twenty-one years?"

"Is that what you want?" he asked gruffly, his hands like heavy weights at his sides.

"Sure is. Don't you?" She stood on tiptoe and kissed him at the side of his mouth. She wanted him to kiss her the way he had this afternoon.

"Are you flirting with me?" he asked sharply.

She laughed, "Is this flirting?" She kissed the other side of his mouth, then his warm lips.

He smelled her skin as he reached to unhook her hands from behind his neck.

Moving closer against him, she nuzzled his neck and tightened her hold.

Her hair tickled his face. Fire leaped in his veins. He wanted to remember his anger and pain, but right now all he could think about was his love for Diane. He wrapped his arms around her and covered her mouth with his hungry lips.

Her heart fluttered, then thudded hard against her rib cage. She returned his kiss hesitantly, then with a growing passion.

He felt her response and kissed her again like he had this afternoon, like he'd wanted to do for as long as he could remember.

She wanted him to say he loved her, but he didn't, and it saddened her. Would he say it to her someday? Would she ever say it to him and mean it?

Suddenly the wind blew the barn door shut with a bang, bringing Seth to his senses. He pulled away from Diane and raked his fingers through his hair. "We've got to get back inside." His voice sounded hoarse and he glanced at Diane. Her hair was tousled and she looked thoroughly kissed. He turned quickly away and lifted down the lantern.

She sighed as she walked beside him down the aisle toward the door. "We'll have to meet like this more often," she said softly as she slipped her hand through his arm.

Seth moved to blow out the lantern and hang it in

place near the door, making her hand fall away. He stepped outdoors and shivered at the blast of icy wind.

She followed him and hunched down in her coat. She still felt warm inside.

He closed the door, dropped the latch in place to lock it, then started for the house.

Diane ran easily beside him and laced her fingers through his.

Against his will he closed his hand over hers and slowed his pace. The moon was bright and beautiful - a lover's moon - but the wind was blowing icy air around them. He had to get her inside before she got too cold without a hat or gloves.

He opened the door and waited for her to walk in. The lamp on the table glowed and the heat wrapped around them.

Macee hurried into the kitchen with Mor in her arms. "He was crying."

Diane slipped off her coat and hung it up. "I thought he'd sleep longer."

"He just now woke up," Macee smiled down at Mor. She had awakened Mor to make sure Diane didn't stay in the kitchen while she talked with Seth. Macee looked up at Diane. "He's a beautiful baby, Diane."

"Thank you." Diane took Mor and held him close. "Excuse me, please, while I feed him." She smiled at Seth, then hurried to the bedroom.

Macee sat at the table with her hands locked in her lap and waited for Seth to hang up his coat and join her at the table. She already knew what she'd tell him. She and Bobby had talked it over after she'd put Barney to bed.

Seth hung up his coat, fixed the fire, then sat down across the table from Macee. "Macee, why did Bobby come here today?"

Her cheeks bright red, Macee took a deep breath. "I don't think you want to know."

Seth frowned, "Tell me."

Macee laced her icy fingers together in her lap. "He said Diane told him it would be a good day to come visit her because you'd be gone."

The world crashed down on Seth and he couldn't move.

CHAPTER 7

Diane finally laid Mor back in his cradle, then dressed for bed in a soft, warm, pink nightdress embroidered with tiny rose-red flowers and green leaves. She'd heard Macee going upstairs several minutes earlier and had expected Seth to come into the bedroom. But he sat in the rocker in the front room instead. She heard the steady creak of the rocker and frowned. Why wasn't Seth coming to bed? Was he so sorry for kissing her that he'd decided to sleep in the rocking chair?

She slipped her cold feet into her slippers and tied her pink robe around her waist. She scowled down at the tie. How long would it take to get her tiny waist and flat tummy back?

Slowly she walked to the front room and stood near the potbelly stove. Heat radiated from it and flames glowed through the vent in the door. In the dim light she could see Seth with his head back and his hands gripping the arms of the rocker. She was not going to let him sleep in the rocker all night long! Her heart fluttered. Taking all the courage she had, she hurried to him and sank down on his lap. "When are you coming to bed?"

"Don't!" he hissed, pushing her away. How dare she

come cuddling with him after she'd invited Bobby over?

Startled at his reaction, she slipped off his knees and started to fall, but caught herself in time. His rejection sent pain ripping through her. But maybe he'd been asleep and had thought Macee was playing games with him. "It's me, Seth. Why'd you push me away?"

He jumped up, his fists doubled at his sides. His feet were bare and his shirt hung out over his levis. "Can't you ever leave me alone?" he whispered so his voice wouldn't carry upstairs.

Tears pricked her eyes as she stumbled back from him. "What have I done?"

He gripped her arm and hauled her to the bedroom, then closed the heavy oak door with a snap. He set her free as if she had burned him. He folded his arms across his chest and glared at her. "I don't want anyone to hear us. Do you? Or maybe it doesn't matter to you!"

"Seth!" Trembling, she took a step toward him. "What's wrong?"

"As if you don't know!"

"But I don't." From the glow of the lamp she could see the anger on his face.

He jabbed a finger at her. "I know you asked Bobby to come see you today."

"What?" Her voice rose and he shushed her with a look and a finger to his lips.

"Don't try to deny it."

Her head spun. How could Seth think such a thing? "I would never do that, Seth! You know that!"

He shook his head, then pushed his face down close to hers. Fire flashed in his blue eyes. "I don't know any such thing."

She backed away and sank weakly down in the rocking chair. What could she say to make him believe her? Suddenly it came to her. She jumped up and waved her finger at him. "Listen to this, Seth McGraw!"

"Nothing you can say will make a difference." He felt almost sick enough to lose his supper.

"Listen! I mean it!" She caught his arm. "Today is Worth's birthday. I would never, ever miss Worth's birthday. We've been planning on going to his birthday celebration for weeks. Isn't that right?"

Seth grudgingly nodded, but he wouldn't let hope spring up inside him.

"I couldn't have told Bobby to come here today because I knew you'd be gone. I knew we'd *both* be gone!"

Seth slowly nodded, frowned, then shook his head as if to clear it. "Why would Macee lie to me?"

"So, *she* told you I said that?"

"Yes."

Diane whirled around and stared at the closed bedroom door. She wanted to storm upstairs and toss Macee out on her ear. "We've been getting along so well! Why would she tell such a terrible lie?"

"Yes. Why?" Seth sank to the edge of the bed. "Something is going on. But what?"

Diane stepped close to Seth and lowered her voice to just above a whisper. "I don't know why Macee would lie to you, but she did. You believe me, don't you?"

"Yes," Seth whispered. He jumped up. "I'm going to kick her out right now!"

"Wait! It's cold and dark." Diane gripped Seth's arm. She knew he meant what he said. If he did kick Macee out, he'd feel guilty immediately. "What about sweet little

Barney?"

Seth's muscles jumped but he nodded. "You're right. I won't toss them out."

"Good! It'll give us a chance to find out why she lied."

Seth frowned thoughtfully. Maybe it was because Macee was jealous of Diane and Bobby. But it could be something entirely different. "I don't think we should let her know that we suspect anything."

"Why?"

"Because we might learn the whole truth. Besides, you need help with the chores so we might as well let Macee work."

Diane tossed her head and her blonde hair shimmered in the light. "I can manage on my own!"

"Not with Bobby here and the extra work he makes."

Diane sighed, "You're right."

Seth glanced at Mor asleep in the cradle and almost asked Diane about Mor and Bobby, but couldn't bring himself to say the words aloud. It would be too painful.

Diane pushed back her hair. "We'd better get to bed. I'll bank the fires."

"I already did."

Diane smiled, "Good. I really didn't want to." She hated stacking the wood just right inside the stoves so they'd burn slowly all night long. She started to kick off her slippers and Mor cried. She waited, hoping he'd go back to sleep, but he cried harder. "I can't see how he can be hungry. Maybe he needs to be burped." She lifted him up and held him to her shoulder. He smelled wet and she knew she'd have to change him again.

Much later she put Mor back to bed, blew out the lamp, and wearily climbed into bed beside Seth. He was sleeping soundly. She curled up against his back to get warm and immediately fell asleep.

The next morning just after daybreak Seth walked into the pasture with the bullwhip over his shoulder. His breath hung in the icy air. Snow had fallen during the night, covering the bare spots. The whole world seemed white.

Pictures of Diane curled up tightly against him flashed across his mind. It had been next to impossible to leave her this morning, but he'd forced himself to get dressed, fix the fires, and step out into the icy world.

Corralling his mind back to the job at hand, he looked around for the bull, but didn't see it. Macee had told Diane Bobby's horse, Spade, was in the pasture. If so, why hadn't Spade been waiting at the fence near the barn where he'd know there was food and water? If for some reason Spade was tied up, he'd have to find him and get him to the barn.

Several minutes later Seth rounded a hill and spotted Spade tied to a lone tree, his head down and his saddle still on. A gunbelt and holster with a .44 in it was draped around the saddlehorn and was powdered with snow. Seth's jaw tightened with anger at the thought of Spade spending an entire night tied up without food and water. Why would Bobby tie Spade there? Didn't he want anyone to know he'd come to the ranch? If that was the reason, why wouldn't he want anyone to know? Bobby had never cared about the gossip around the community concerning him.

Spade lifted his head and nickered, his breath freezing in the air.

Seth held his hand out to Spade, then patted his neck. "Had a rough night? I'll take you to the barn, big feller."

Spade blew out his breath and bobbed his head.

"I know you're tired of standing there. And you're hungry and thirsty." Seth talked to Spade as he tightened the cinch strap, brushed snow off the saddle and holster with his gloved hand, then mounted easily. Spade danced uneasily, then quieted. Seth nudged Spade with his knees and headed back for the ranch yard.

Seth broke a hole in the crust of ice in the big wooden tank, watered Spade, then led him inside, unsaddled him and put him in a stall. Red whinnied and Spade answered. Seth poured grain in a low bucket and forked hay into the manger. He fed and watered Red, milked the cow, and hurried to the chicken house to feed and water the chickens and gather eggs. The chickens cackled and flapped their wings as Seth poured cracked corn into the feeder. He broke the ice out of the watering trough and refilled it with fresh water. Dust rose around him and feathers flew as he lifted the warm eggs out of the row of nests nailed to the wall. Just as he started out of the chicken house he saw Macee running toward the pasture fence, her skirts flapping about her ankles. He frowned. What was she doing? Going after Spade?

Seth set the basket of eggs beside the bucket of milk and hurried after her, calling, "Macee! Wait! There's a bull in the pasture."

Macee turned, her face red, then walked back to Seth. She didn't know what to say. She'd thought Seth was in the barn.

Seth forced a smile. "I got Spade and put him inside a stall. Tell Bobby he's all right."

Macee smiled, but her nerves were as tight as the strings on her pa's fiddle. "He was worried about Spade. Thanks."

"Tell him he doesn't have to worry about Spade." Seth watched Macee's reaction, but she was good at hiding her feelings.

"I will." Macee didn't know what to think of Seth. She knew the lies Bobby had told Seth about Diane. How could he set aside his feelings to help Bobby?

Seth fell into step beside Macee as they walked toward the house. "After I take care of the milk and eggs, I'll carry water in to heat for doing the washing."

"Thank you."

"Bobby's clothes are filthy. It's a wonder the bull didn't kill him."

Macee shuddered, "It's a good thing you found him." She had to change the subject before she burst into tears at Bobby's close call. "Diane's still asleep."

"Good. Mor kept her up late last night."

"I remember how that was with Barney." Macee glanced up at Seth, "Did you eat yet?"

"No."

"I'll make breakfast for you."

"I'd appreciate it." He didn't want to depend on her for anything, but he didn't let it show. Somehow he had to learn why she'd lied to him about Diane.

In her bedroom Diane dressed slowly in a green wool dress that hung gracefully over her muslin petticoats and touched her black hightop shoes. She brushed her hair until it snapped, then tied a green ribbon around it to hold it off her face. She was hungry enough to eat a plate of eggs, potatoes, and bacon. For the first time since they'd married, she couldn't wait to see Seth. It felt strange to feel excited about seeing the man she'd lived with for nine months.

She made the bed and rested her hand on the pillow where he'd laid his head. She sighed, then pulled the bright quilt in place that covered the blankets. She bent down to Mor and saw he was sleeping soundly. She smiled and kissed her fingers and touched his head. What a precious, wonderful baby!

The house seemed very quiet as she walked to the kitchen. She found it empty, but the fire was burning well. She looked out the window at the snowy yard. Macee and Seth stood together talking earnestly. Diane frowned. Was Seth finding out why Macee had lied last night?

Diane glanced over her shoulder. Maybe this was a good time to talk to Bobby without Macee hovering nearby. Diane hesitated, lifted her skirts a little, and then ran lightly upstairs. She peeked in at Barney to find him still asleep, curled in a ball under his covers. Her heart racing, she stopped at Bobby's open door. Should she run back downstairs without speaking to him?

"Diane," he said weakly as he lifted his head.

She hurried to his side, "How are you this morning?"

"I'll live, I reckon."

"Can I get you something?"

"Let me look at you. You're pretty as a spring flower."

She flushed and her pulse leaped, then she frowned. She dare not let Bobby speak to her that way! She dare not respond to him! "Why were you in our pasture yesterday?"

Bobby thought quickly. What could he say to stop Diane from nosing around? "I came to see you."

"Why didn't you use the road?"

"I took a short cut." Sweat dampened his skin.

"Then why leave Spade in the pasture?"

Bobby had to get her to stop questioning him. He took her hand and held it even as she tried to pull away. "I wanted to see you without McGraw knowing I was here."

Diane yanked her hand away before he felt the flutter of her pulse. "Don't say that!"

"You already know how I feel about you."

Diane gaped down at Bobby. He was lying! She'd seen the way he looked at Macee. Had Bobby always lied to her about his feelings like Maureen had said? Diane wanted to shout for Bobby to be truthful with her, but she pushed the words back. She had to know the real reason he'd come to the ranch. Finally she said, "Do you want breakfast?"

"Yes, but I want to go downstairs to eat."

"I'll have Seth help you down."

Bobby shook his head. He didn't want Seth to do anything for him. "Don't bother."

"He won't mind."

Bobby's jaw tightened. He didn't want Seth touching him! "I'm going back to Stone's ranch today."

"You're still too sore."

"I don't care. I'm going."

Diane shrugged, "It's your decision, but you're welcome to stay longer."

"Did McGraw say that?"

"Yes."

Guilt washed over Bobby. He had to leave before he got as religious as Diane and Seth and broke down and confessed the lies he'd told Seth. "I want to get more sleep before I head out."

"I'll send Seth up later."

"No!" Bobby lifted his head again. "Get my clothes so I can go."

"They're dirty. We're going to wash them today, but after they're dry, you can have them. You could wear something of Seth's, but all of his things are dirty too." Diane laughed and rolled her eyes. "Having a baby has put me behind on my work. That's why Macee is here. To help me." Diane headed for the door, then turned back. She wanted to get Bobby to admit his feelings for Macee. "I'm pleased Macee was free to come help us. It's too bad about her husband."

"Sure is. Did you know him?"

"No. I know Barney misses him."

"He's a good kid."

"Macee adores him."

"I noticed."

Diane cleared her throat, excused herself, and hurried away. She reached the bottom step just as Seth and Macee walked in.

Macee was saying, "So, don't tell Diane what I said last night, Seth. I don't want her angry with me."

Diane stiffened as she waited for Seth's answer.

"Whatever you say, Macee," Seth said.

Diane smiled. They'd learn the truth from Macee and Bobby as long as they worked together.

Flipping her hair, Diane hurried into the kitchen. "Good morning! Is it cold out?"

"Icy," Seth said as he readied the clean bucket to strain the milk into.

"It snowed a little last night," Macee said as she hung her coat and bonnet on a peg near the door.

"I was just upstairs to see if Bobby's ready for breakfast. He'd like to come downstairs."

Macee gasped, "I'll see about that! He's not strong

enough!" She hurried away, her blue eyes flashing.

Diane waited until Macee was all the way upstairs, then stepped close to Seth and whispered, "Why was she out-doors?"

"To get Spade." Seth frowned and shook his head, then told Diane where he'd found Spade. "I can't understand why Bobby would leave Spade in the pasture. He loves that horse! Why not ride him right up to the door? Or put him in the barn if he wanted him out of sight?"

"It's a mystery all right," Diane giggled. "Maureen would like solving it." Just then Diane remembered what Maureen had said about Seth. "If I were married to him, I'd love him with my whole heart." Diane's heart swelled as she watched Seth finished straining the milk into a clean container. The feeling took her by surprise and she turned away. Could she really learn to love him with her whole heart? It made her feel strange to think of loving Seth with the passion Ma had for Pa. But what if she loved him passionately and he was still cold and indifferent to her like he'd been most of their married life?

Abruptly she pushed the thought aside. She was to love Seth no matter what he thought of her. How would it feel to long for his touch? Hang on his every word? Yearn to hear his thoughts and dreams?

The thoughts were so new to her that she had to walk away from him. She peered out the window, but didn't see the snow or the buildings. She saw Seth's red hair, freckles, bold blue eyes, lean body, and strong hands. She once again felt his passionate kisses and she trembled.

Seth watched Diane and frowned. What was she think-ing? Was she upset because Macee was alone with Bobby? Seth set the bucket down on the wooden floor with a clatter.

How much more could he take? God had promised he wouldn't give him more than he could bear. But he couldn't bear Diane loving Bobby! But that hadn't been God's doing.

His heart heavy, Seth grabbed the water bucket. "I'll get fresh water." He rushed to the well to fill it. "Heavenly Father, I need your help right now! I can't stand to see Diane love Bobby instead of me!" Seth vigorously pumped water into the bucket while he continued to pray. In his heart he heard, "Love her unconditionally."

Seth stopped stock still, his hands on the cold pump handle. "Love her?" he whispered. But he did love her. How could he love her more? He knew the Scripture that said a husband was to love his wife as Christ loved the church. Christ loved unconditionally.

Seth bowed his head. Did he love Diane unconditionally? Would he love her even if she continued to love Bobby? Would he love her even if Mor was Bobby's? Would he love her if she never got back her tiny waist? Or if she never cooked a good meal for him again? Or if she never washed his clothes? Would he love her if she never returned his love? Seth groaned from deep inside.

Just then Maureen rode into the yard astraddle Morgan's dapple gray mare. "Seth!" Maureen jumped to the ground beside him, flicked her dark green riding skirt down in place and retied the bow of her matching bonnet. Her cheeks were red and her brown eyes sparkled. "I thought you'd like to hear the latest gossip."

"What is it?" Maureen was more excitable than any of the Clements family and it made Seth chuckle. The most mundane thing could be a great adventure to Maureen.

"Bobby Ryder is missing!"

"What?" Seth stepped away from the pump.

"The gossip is that Julius Goddard killed him because he couldn't pay his gambling debt. I came to speak to Macee Caulder to see what she knows about it."

Seth tensed, "Why would she know anything?"

"She was trying to find a way to help him pay off his debt. Maybe he ran off. Maybe Goddard didn't kill him."

Seth's head whirled with Maureen's information. "What'll you do if you find Bobby?"

Maureen giggled and leaned toward Seth. "Use Bobby to get evidence against Julius Goddard so the sheriff can put him in jail or run him out of town."

"You're not the law, Maureen."

"As good as! I'm a newspaper woman!" Her voice rang proudly across the yard and off into the vast prairie.

"You're quite a girl."

Maureen giggled and wrinkled her nose. "I know."

"Did Worth get off all right this morning?"

Maureen's smile dimmed. "Yes. I'll miss him a lot! But, oh, I envy him getting to go!"

"I'm glad for him, but I don't envy him a bit. I'm thankful for what I have right here."

Just then Diane ran out the door, shouting, "Maureen! What a surprise to see you!"

Maureen ran to Diane and they hugged as if they hadn't seen each other in weeks instead of only a day.

"You're just in time for breakfast. Have you eaten?"

"Before dawn, but I'm hungry again." Maureen turned back to Seth. "Let's go eat, shall we?"

"I'm ready." He picked up the bucket of water and followed Maureen and Diane inside. Smells of biscuits, eggs, bacon, and coffee filled the warm kitchen.

"I am really hungry!" Maureen cried as she slipped out of her jacket and lifted off her bonnet. "Where's Macee? Isn't she eating with us?"

Diane started to say she was upstairs with Bobby, but she caught a look from Seth and knew to keep the information to herself. "She'll be down later."

"I have questions to ask her." Maureen washed and dried her hands, then sat where Diane told her to.

Seth washed, then sat at his usual place. After Diane was seated Seth asked the blessing on the food. Before Maureen could start gossip about Bobby, Seth said, "Maureen said Worth got off just fine this morning, Diane."

"That's wonderful." Diane handed the plate of eggs to Maureen. "Tell me every detail! How was he dressed? Was he excited or nervous? Was the stage on time? What other passengers were there?"

Maureen answered all the questions as they ate. Seth kept her off the subject of Bobby and the gambler until he could sort things out and talk to Diane privately to see what she thought. If Maureen discovered Bobby was there, maybe they'd never learn the truth from Bobby or Macee. Everyone knew Maureen's tongue wagged at both ends. Everyone knew much of what she learned and prattled on about ended up in the newspaper because there wasn't any other news to fill the pages. The readers could take just so much politics and news of folks in other parts of the world.

Just then Mor cried. Diane jumped up to get him, but Seth caught her hand. "I think Aunt Maureen would like to get Mor." Seth turned to Maureen. "Wouldn't you?"

Diane stared down at Seth's strong hand holding hers. It did funny things to her heartbeat.

Maureen's face glowed. "Yes, I would! I'll be back in

a minute."

"You can change his diaper in the bedroom, if you want," Seth said. "Clean diapers are in his chest near his cradle."

Diane was speechless. What was going on?

"I'll find them." Maureen hurried away, her boots loud on the floor.

Seth tugged Diane away from the doorway as far away as possible.

The touch of his hand on hers sent her pulse leaping.

"Maureen came looking for Bobby."

Diane gasped.

Seth quickly told Diane what Maureen had said. "I don't want her to learn Bobby's here or she'll spread it all over the paper, then we'll never find out why he came."

"Wasn't it to see Macee?"

"Could be. But he wouldn't hide Spade if that was all there was to it."

"You're probably right. What'll we do to keep her from talking to Macee?"

"I'll tell Macee not to say anything to Maureen about Bobby being here. I don't think she'll question me. She wouldn't want anyone to know he's here, especially if what Maureen said about the gambler is right."

Diane flung her arms around Seth and kissed him full on the lips. "I like working with you."

Seth's blood thundered in his veins. He wrapped his arms around her and returned her kiss in unrestrained passion. At the sound of footsteps he quickly dropped his arms and turned away.

Diane's heart raced as she tried to act as if she hadn't just been thoroughly kissed.

CHAPTER 8

Just as Macee walked into the kitchen Seth grabbed her coat and his and ushered her outdoors to warn her not to tell Maureen that Bobby was there and why.

Chills ran up and down Macee's spine. Was Seth kicking her out?

When the door closed behind them, Diane breathed a sigh of relief, then hurried to the bedroom to talk to Maureen. She was sitting in the rocking chair, talking to Mor. Diane smiled at the pretty picture they made together. "Isn't he the most adorable baby in the world?"

Maureen giggled, "In our small part of the world." She sobered. "Did you get to have your private talk with Seth?"

Diane flushed.

"You can't fool me." Maureen grinned impishly. "I know he wanted to tell you something that he didn't want me to hear." Maureen giggled, "What was it?"

Diane laughed, "You don't know what you're talking about."

"I'm not a baby, Diane! I know what's going on."

Diane locked her icy hands behind her back. Had she listened at the door to their private conversation the way she did when she wanted a newspaper story? "You do?"

"Of course," Maureen looked very smug. "He's madly, passionately in love with you and he had to tell you right then or burst wide open."

Diane suddenly yearned for that very thing. Just thinking about it sent tingles up and down her spine. Maybe someday it would be true, but it wasn't now. Admitting it to herself depressed her. She forced a laugh. "Maureen, you're such a romantic! I'll enjoy watching you when you fall in love."

"You'll have to wait until I get back from my trip with Ganny!"

"I hope you wait until you're over eighteen." Diane reached for Mor. "Want me to take him?"

Maureen nodded, "He's really hungry. Shall I stay in here and talk to you, or go to the kitchen with Seth?"

"It doesn't matter." Diane sat down with Mor to her breast. She looked up at Maureen who was looking out the bedroom window. "How long are you staying?"

Maureen turned with a smile. "Not long. Ganny expects me back yet this morning."

"When is she leaving on her trip?"

"March or April. She hasn't decided."

"I wish you wouldn't go." Diane bit her lip and shook her head. "I'm sorry. I know you want to go, so do it and be happy!"

"Thanks, I will." Maureen grinned as she sank to the edge of the bed, her hands on either side of her, her divided riding skirt brushing the tops of her boots. "I'm glad you aren't trying to make me feel guilty so I'll stay home."

"Me too," Diane sighed heavily. "I honestly didn't know I did that, but I did. I'm sorry."

Maureen shrugged, "That's all right. I knew you'd

change."

"How'd you know that?" Diane lifted her fine brows questioningly.

Maureen spread her slender, graceful hands wide. "God answers prayer."

"You're right." Smiling, Diane lifted Mor to her shoulder and patted his back. His head bobbed around, then steadied against her.

Maureen absently rocked the cradle with the toe of her boot. "I saw Ord Williams yesterday. What a waste, Di!"

"He's been the town drunk as long as I can remember. I don't know how Janice puts up with it."

Maureen's face hardened. "Ord's been gambling too. Janice is mad! Maybe mad enough to shoot Julius Goddard." Maureen leaned forward with an earnest look on her face. "At times I wish she'd do it! She works hard from dawn 'til dark for money to keep food on their table and Ord drinks and gambles it away. I think it's awful!"

"So do I!"

"Ganny is ready to shoot Julius Goddard herself. He's ruined too many lives!" Maureen told of Abe Peabody who had gambled away his team of mules and lost his freight business because of it and Lincoln Engersol who'd gambled away money for the bank payment on his ranch. "They and their wives are ready to string Goddard up! Linc would've lost the ranch if Graham Santclair hadn't given him more time to pay the loan."

"I'm surprised Mr. Santclair was so nice. I remember one time Pa was behind on a payment and almost lost his place."

Maureen gasped, "I didn't know that!"

"Nick Stone helped him out."

They talked longer as Diane finished nursing Mor.

Maureen jumped up. "I almost forgot to tell you - Kate said she was coming to see you tomorrow afternoon unless it snows."

"Good!" Then Diane remembered Bobby Ryder upstairs and her heart sank. It would be very hard to keep Bobby's presence a secret from Kate Mayberry.

"What's the matter? Don't you want to see Kate?"

"Yes, of course!"

"She won't mind catching you in the middle of doing the wash."

"How'd you know I was going to do the wash?"

"Seth said you and Macee were going to do it." Maureen wrinkled her nose at the pile of Mor's soiled clothes. "This room will smell better once you get those things clean."

"You can stay to help if you want."

"No, thanks. You can have the pleasure of being a housewife and mother. I am a newspaper woman!"

Diane laughed as she laid Mor in his cradle and covered him warmly. "Let's go to the kitchen, newspaper woman, and let Mor sleep."

Later Maureen rode away, not getting any information from Macee.

His brow furrowed in thought, Seth stood in the yard and watched until she was a black dot in the vast whiteness. Maybe he should've told Maureen that Bobby was there so Julius Goddard could find him and kill him.

"No!" Seth's cry rang out across the prairie. He would not allow the devil to tempt him to sin! Pushing aside thoughts of Bobby, Seth hurried to the barn to work with Red Lightning.

While the water heated for doing the washing, Diane

sorted the clothes. Macee filled the lamps with kerosene, trimmed the wicks with scissors, washed and dried the chimneys, then set them back in place.

Macee held up a lamp. Inside the glass base the wick curled in the dull yellow kerosene. The glass chimney sparkled. "I always like to see a newly cleaned chimney gleam bright." A sad look filled her eyes. "I wish life could be that way - a bright gleaming look after a good washing."

Diane looked up from checking Seth's shirt pockets. She couldn't pass up the opportunity to say, "Jesus can do that for you. I know you heard that when you went to church as a girl. The blood of Jesus washes away sin and makes you white as snow."

"Oh, that!" Macee wrinkled her nose, but inside she yearned to hear more. She wanted the peace brought only by accepting Jesus as her personal Savior, but if she gave in, she'd lose Bobby. He'd already told her he would never get what he called "religion."

"Jesus loves you, Macee."

"I don't want to hear it, Diane." Macee carried two lamps to the front room before Diane could say more.

Silently praying for Macee, Diane finished sorting the clothes. She checked Seth's levi pockets and found a few coins, several matches, a red bandana, and a folded scrap of paper. She unfolded the paper to find a line drawing of the buggy Seth had built for Nick Stone. At the bottom corner of the paper was a heart with her name written on it. Diane's pulse jumped. She ran a finger lightly over the heart and her name, then quickly tucked the paper in her apron pocket to look at later when she knew Macee wouldn't walk in on her.

Diane pushed aside a pile of towels. A heart with "Diane" written on it! Could it mean Seth loved her? Or was it just idle doodling? She touched the paper in her pocket and it crackled. They were no longer school children, so why think the way a schoolgirl thought?

Impatiently she set up the tub and washboard, shaved soap from the bar into the tub, then filled it with scalding water. She used a stick to push Mor's clothes down into the water. Steam rose up around her along with the biting odor of wet diapers. She laid the stick against the tub, picked up the wooden plunger and sloshed it up and down in the clothes as suds billowed up around the plunger handle. Her back and arms ached from lifting up and pushing down. Finally she reached in with the stick and lifted up a diaper. Water ran from it down into the sudsy tub. She gingerly took the scalding hot diaper and wrung it out, then dropped it in the tub of rinse water. When the washtub was empty she put in the next load. Macee used the plunger while Diane rinsed and wrung out Mor's diapers and shirts, then hung them over a line stretched from one corner of the kitchen to another. She would hang most of the other clothes outdoors on the line to let them flap dry in the cold wind. She shivered at the thought of the icy wind on her wet hands. She always came back inside with red hands and a red nose.

By the time the clothes were washed, the water was black and cold. Seth emptied it outdoors a bucketful at a time. It left a wet patch in the snow.

At suppertime clothes still hung on the kitchen lines. Macee fried potatoes together with beef Diane had canned in the fall. The smell made Diane's stomach growl with hunger as she sat in her bedroom nursing Mor. Barney was singing "Nellie Bly" at the top of his lungs as he watched for Seth at the kitchen window. Diane laughed softly as she burped Mor. Someday, would he sing at the top of his lungs while he waited for Seth?

The paper in her apron pocket crackled and she eased it out and looked at it. When had Seth drawn the heart with her name in it? Had he done it at the kitchen table when he was all alone? Or had it been before Mor was born when she was busy around the house and he was at the table working on the plans for the buggy? She pushed it back in her pocket and smiled.

When Mor was finally finished, Diane laid him back in his cradle and covered him up. She brushed her hair and retied the ribbon. She frowned into her looking glass. How tired she looked! Would Seth notice and think she was old and ugly? Sighing, she turned away from the looking glass and walked out of the bedroom.

Bobby stood on the stairs, his face white.

"Bobby!" Diane ran to him. "What're you doing? You should've called down for Seth to help you."

Bobby scowled and wiped sweat off his upper lip. He felt like he'd been kicked from one side of the county to another, but he was not going to accept help from Seth McGraw. "I can make it down by myself."

Her hair in tangles, Macee ran up the stairs. She looked bone weary. "Bobby, get back to bed!"

He brushed her aside. "I'm going downstairs, so don't try to stop me."

Diane sighed and walked back down, but Macee stayed at Bobby's side until he reached a kitchen chair.

Bobby leaned back in the chair with a tired sigh. Walking downstairs had been as tiring as a full day's work.

His eyes wide, Barney stood close to Bobby. "Ma says you won't die."

Bobby grinned. "I won't. Not right now, at least."

Macee swatted at Barney's bottom. "Hush! Leave Bobby alone."

"It's all right." Bobby ruffled Barney's dark hair. "I heard you singing. You get yourself a guitar and learn to ride a horse and you can be a real cowboy just like me."

"Yipee!" Barney raced around the kitchen on an imaginary horse, ducking clothes and furniture.

Macee frowned at Bobby. "Barney can work on a ranch while he's growing up, but he's going to make something of himself when he's out of school. I'll see to that!"

Diane felt self-conscious listening and watching Bobby and Macee. She was glad when Seth walked in, bringing in the smell of fresh, cold air. Snow fell from his boots and skittered across the floor. The paper in her pocket seemed to weigh more than a bucket of water. She managed to smile at Seth, then blushed.

"How's Spade?" Bobby asked sharply.

Seth set the milk and eggs down. "He's just fine. I let him out in the corral for a while today for exercise. He acts like he's not used to being locked in a stall all day."

"He's not," Bobby cleared his throat. "Thanks for tending him." It was mighty hard to get the words out, but it was only right.

"It's nothing." Seth turned away and strained the milk. He didn't like seeing Bobby in his kitchen at his table.

"I'll be out of your way tomorrow. I'm leaving early in the morning."

Seth glanced at Diane's reaction to Bobby's statement, but she didn't have one. Seth almost dropped the bucket. Didn't Diane mind that Bobby was leaving?

Macee bit back a sharp cry as she dropped down on a chair next to Bobby. "Wait another day. Please, Bobby!"

"Can I go with you?" Barney asked as he clasped Bobby's hand.

Bobby laughed. "How could you go with me, Barn? I live in a bunk house with a bunch of cowboys."

"I could be a cowboy with you! I could learn how to ride a horse and play a guitar and spit like you do."

Everyone laughed and Barney ducked his head, then raced around the room, laughing and singing hard. Macee caught him and demanded he sit down and be quiet.

"Sit by me and tell me a story, Barn," Bobby said with a grin.

Macee frowned at Bobby, then turned away to put supper on the table. She didn't like to have Bobby spoil Barney. She wanted him to grow to be a fine man - like Seth McGraw.

Diane set glasses on the table. "Who wants milk besides me and Barney?"

"Me," Bobby said.

Macee set a mug on the table. "Coffee for me, please."

"I'll have water," Seth said as he washed his hands in the washpan on the stand near the door. He combed his hair, scowled at his reflection in the looking glass, then turned away from it. He needed a haircut. Laurel had cut it the last two times. Maybe she would again. He glanced at Diane as she sat at the table. Maybe she'd cut it. His stomach did flip-flops at the thought of her touching his hair, combing it, cutting it. No, he couldn't handle having her cut it. It was getting harder and harder to keep his hands off her. He frowned slightly. But why should he? She was his wife. Just then she laughed at something Bobby said and Seth's blood turned cold again.

After supper while they still sat around the table Diane

suddenly thought of her diary. She had to ask Bobby about it. And why not do it right in front of Seth? Fear pricked her. She took a deep breath and turned to Bobby. "I was thinking about my mother's diary that I carried to school with me in sixth grade."

Bobby's heart sank, but he didn't let it show. "What diary?"

Seth wanted to take Bobby apart, but he didn't move. He watched Diane carefully. She probably had to hear the truth from Bobby before she'd believe it.

Diane frowned, "You know what diary! You took it from my desk, hid it in the woodpile, and laughed about it. When the teacher insisted the culprit give it back to me, Seth found it and started to return it to me, but you grabbed it and told me you found it. And that Seth had stolen it."

Bobby felt hot all over, but he shook his head and looked innocent. "I don't remember that at all."

Macee frowned. She'd heard about the diary, but hadn't heard the truth until now.

"I know you remember," Diane said sharply. "I want to know why you'd do that to me."

Bobby shrugged and shook his head. "I honestly don't remember it, Diane. It was a schoolboy prank. I sure can't remember all my pranks."

Diane suddenly wanted to slap Bobby, but she locked her hands in her lap. Why couldn't he at least admit what he'd done? She looked helplessly at Seth.

He saw her look and tried to think of something to say. Finally he said, "I remember it. I'm glad you got it back."

She smiled, "Thanks."

"Do you still have it?" Macee asked.

Diane nodded. "I have it put away for my daughter -

when we have one."

Abruptly Seth pushed back his chair. "I better check on the horses again and get a fresh pail of water." He could not listen to Diane speak so innocently and easily about having a daughter while Bobby was sitting there.

Diane frowned slightly. Seth really did get upset when she mentioned having more children. But why?

Bobby absently played with his fork. "My ma never kept a diary. She didn't know how to write. That's why she was so set on me getting book learning."

"I'm glad she did," Macee said with a nod. "Barney's going to have more schooling than we had. I even want him to go to college."

Bobby whistled, "That's high ambitions, ain't it?"

Macee flushed, "Yes, but that's my plan for him."

Diane looked thoughtfully toward the bedroom where Mor was sleeping peacefully. She hadn't thought about his schooling. But she wanted him to have a good education. Pa had said a time was coming when all children would have to have a high school education if they wanted to make their way in life.

The next morning Diane stood to one side and watched Bobby slip on his coat and hat. His clothes were clean and Macee had ironed them neatly. Colored bruises covered his face. Thread spiked out a line down his cheek. Barney and Macee were putting on their coats too. "Take care of yourself, Bobby," Diane said.

Bobby flushed and nodded. He had to get out of this house fast! How could Seth and Diane be nice to him after what he'd done and what he still planned to do to them? "See you around," he said gruffly. He flung open the door and rushed out with Macee and Barney right behind him.

Diane waited for a sense of loss to hit her at Bobby's going, but none came. She stood at the window as Macee and Barney walked to the barn with Bobby to get Spade. Seth had ridden out to check cattle and had said he wouldn't be back until late. He'd told Bobby a stilted goodbye.

A few minutes later Bobby rode into sight on Spade. Bobby held Barney in front of him on the saddle. At the porch he eased him down to stand beside Macee who was brushing tears from her eyes.

Diane looked past Bobby on Spade and off in the direction Seth had ridden. She had wanted to show Seth the paper she carried in her pocket, but couldn't find the courage in case he said it meant nothing.

Finally Bobby rode away and Macee walked back inside. Her eyes and the tip of her nose were red. "I told Barney he could play outside. He's got too much energy to stay inside."

"He's full of life all right." Diane filled the dishpan with hot water and did the dishes while Macee ironed the clothes with flat irons she heated on the stove.

"He said he'd come see me tomorrow," Macee said in a strangled voice.

Diane looked up from rubbing at a blob of dried egg on a plate. "You love him, don't you?"

Macee sighed, "Yes. I don't want to though."

"Because he doesn't want responsibility?"

"Yes!" Macee suddenly wanted to tell Diane about Bobby's terrible plan to steal Red Lightning and give her to Julius Goddard for payment of his gambling debt, but she bit back the appalling confession. She'd planned to help Bobby, but had told him this morning she wouldn't help him no matter how hard he begged or how angry he got at her.

It had been a hard decision to make, but she made it for Barney's sake. He had to make something of himself, but how could he if his momma was a common thief?

Diane heard the admission of Macee's love, but it didn't bother her at all. She bent over the dishpan and hid a smile. At last she was free of Bobby Ryder!

In the middle of the afternoon Kate Mayberry drove in, climbed from the buggy, and tied her horse near the porch at the hitchrail.

Diane grabbed her coat and ran outdoors to greet her. Icy wind bit into Diane and she shivered. The fresh air felt good after being cooped up inside baking bread and churning butter. "Kate!"

Kate hugged Diane, then stepped back. Kate's cheeks were red and her eyes flashed with excitement. "I just heard the most dreadful news!"

Diane's stomach cramped. "What is it?"

"Somebody found Julius Goddard shot to death early this morning. Sheriff Prescott arrested Bobby Ryder and put him in jail just before I left town."

Diane's eyes widened, "When was Goddard shot?"

"I saw him last night, so it had to be after that and before six this morning."

Diane waved her hand to brush aside the accusation. "Then Bobby didn't do it."

"How do you know?"

"He was here."

"Here?" Kate stared at Diane in shock. "How could you have him here, Diane? What on earth did Seth say about that?"

"Come inside and I'll tell you the whole story." Diane led Kate inside and hung her coat on a peg. Warmth wrapped around them. Diane turned to Macee. "Kate has news you'll want to hear. But sit down first."

"Bobby's shot!" Macee cried as she dropped to a chair, her face ashen.

Diane frowned in surprise. "No! Where'd you get that idea?"

Macee pressed her hand to her heart. Goddard had said he'd shoot Bobby if he didn't pay his debt. "Then what?"

Kate looked helplessly at Diane, then turned to Macee. "Julius Goddard was shot and killed early this morning. The sheriff arrested Bobby for it just as I was leaving town."

"Arrested Bobby? But that's impossible! Tell her, Diane!"

"I already did."

Macee leaped to her feet. "I have to get to town! I must tell the sheriff Bobby was here!" She walked in circles, her head spinning.

Diane caught Macee's arm. "Calm yourself, Macee. Get your things while Kate and I get your horse and buggy. Take some clothes with you in case you want to stay in town."

"Yes. Stay in town. I'll get Barney and be ready right away."

Several minutes later she rode away with Barney beside her, the buggy swaying dangerously.

Kate shook her head as she stood at the window with Diane. "She's crazy in love with Bobby, isn't she?"

"Yes," Diane smiled, pleased the knowledge didn't cause even a flicker of pain.

"I wonder if Barney really is Bobby's son."

"I think so," Diane said softly. "Barney's a great kid. It's too bad Bobby can't grow up and enjoy him." Even as she said it, pain stabbed Diane. Why couldn't Seth enjoy his son? He was very mature, yet he ignored his own baby. Somehow she had to learn the truth from him.

"I saw Alane at the school during noon recess." Kate poured a cup of coffee and sat at the table. "She asked me to mail a letter for her."

Diane gasped, "Where to?"

"A rancher in South Dakota."

Diane dropped down beside Kate. "Did you mail it?"

Kate nodded, "I tried to talk her out of it, but she was determined. She is really afraid she'll be an old maid like me." Kate's eyes filled with tears. "I hate being an old maid!"

Just then Diane smelled the bread and knew it was done. As she listened to Kate talk about herself and Alane, Diane opened the oven and let out heat with the strong aroma of fresh bread. She pulled the pans out of the oven and turned the loaves out onto a clean dishtowel on the table. She buttered the golden brown top crust, making it shiny, and left the loaves to cool. Again she sat down beside Kate and took her hand. "Kate, maybe it's time you started looking at other men. Garrett isn't ready for marriage yet."

Kate shook her head. "He's the only man for me, Di. The only man!"

They talked about Garrett for a while, then Diane sighed and said, "Alane said she wouldn't send that letter until she talked to me."

"That's what she said when she gave it to me to mail, but she felt she couldn't wait any longer. She told me to tell you in case she couldn't see you until Sunday at church."

"I don't want her to marry without love!" Diane jumped up and paced the kitchen. "She could be without love her whole life! Then what? Love is as important as food and shelter! More important!"

"I know," Kate whispered.

The door opened and Seth walked in. "Howdy, Kate," he said with a welcoming smile as he slipped off his hat and coat. Then he frowned. "Where's Macee and Barney?"

Diane and Kate quickly told Seth what had happened.

"You'll have to go into town and tell the sheriff Bobby was here," Diane said, her eyes wide.

Seth froze. Why should he once again save Bobby's life? "You said Macee went to tell the sheriff."

"But he might not believe her!" Diane cried.

Kate nodded. "The gossip around town is Macee's in love with Bobby and would do anything for him."

"I'll think about it." Seth poured himself a cup of hot coffee and sat at the table across from Diane. He wrapped his icy hands around the steaming mug. Let Bobby rot in jail!

Diane frowned, "Seth, he's innocent! You must help him!"

"I can stay with Diane and Mor until you get back," Kate said. "I know you don't want them to be alone, especially if you have to stay in town for the night."

"Macee will take care of Bobby," Seth said impatiently.

Diane was quiet a while, then stated firmly, "Seth, if you don't go, then I will!"

Seth's jaw tightened. He knew Diane meant what she said. She'd bundle Mor up and go to town no matter how cold it was or how long the drive.

"The sheriff will listen to me."

Seth sighed heavily. "I reckon it looks like I'll have to go help Bobby."

Her cheeks flushed, Diane jumped up. "I don't want to stay behind! I'll go to town with you, Seth. Mor and I will!"

Seth moved in agitation. "We won't get back 'til dark."

"I don't care!" Diane rushed to the bedroom to get Mor's things packed.

His face dark with anger, Seth paced the kitchen. How could he talk Diane out of going? If he ordered her to stay home, she'd climb in the buggy and go anyway.

Kate watched him, then excused herself and hurried to the bedroom. "Diane, Seth doesn't want you to go. Maybe you'd better stay home."

Diane stopped and stared at Kate in surprise. "Why didn't he say that?"

"You know Seth. He never could speak his mind."

"So I've learned." Diane dropped Mor's pack on the bed. "Wait here, Kate. I want to talk to Seth alone."

"Go easy on him," Kate whispered, then added with a giggle, "he's only a man, you know. He can't take your sharp tongue."

Diane rushed out of the room, then stopped. She would not be sharp with Seth! If she was, he'd never tell her why he didn't want her to go. She took a deep breath and walked into the kitchen slowly.

Seth stopped his pacing and faced her, his eyes watchful.

"Maybe it would be better if you go alone, Seth." She laced her fingers together. "Do you think so?"

He stared at Diane as if he hadn't seen her before. "I thought you were determined to go no matter how I felt."

She stepped close to him and laid her hands on his chest. "I'm sorry. I didn't mean to do that. You tell me what you want."

His heart thundered under her hands. "I want you to stay home. It's cold out. Besides, the jail is no place for you. I'll deal with the sheriff."

Diane bit back her argument and nodded. Suddenly she wanted to do what Seth wanted her to do, not what she wanted. She took a deep breath. "If that's what you want, that's what I'll do."

Seth's face softened. Had he heard her correctly? "Spoken like a true wife," he whispered.

She smiled as she slid her arms around his neck. "I am a true wife."

His pulse racing, he bent his head and kissed her.

She closed her eyes and laced her fingers through the thickness of his hair as she returned his kiss. Maybe now he'd say the words, *I love you.* She stayed in his arms, but he never spoke the words.

He stepped away from her and said briskly, "I'll head on out and be back as soon as I can."

"I'll do the chores if you're not back in time."

He frowned, "I reckon you'll have to, but I don't like it a bit. Maybe Kate should stay and help you."

"That's not necessary. Her pa needs her worse." Diane touched the paper in her pocket and thought of the kiss Seth had just given her. Was it possible he loved her and just couldn't say the words?

CHAPTER 9

At the outskirts of Broken Arrow near a couple of huge naked cottonwood trees Seth stopped Prancer and drooped in the saddle. On both sides and behind him were snow-covered rolling hills and the town lay out in front of him - gray buildings against the white background of winter. Cold wind burned the skin on his face, blending his freckles together. His sheepskin-lined leather coat and cotton longjohns kept the rest of him warm. He scowled. He should've stayed home. "I won't help Bobby again," Seth muttered. "Let the sheriff hang him!"

Suddenly a shot rang out, whistled past Seth's head, and was lost in the prairie. With an urgent prayer Seth jerked his rifle from the scabbard at the side of the saddle, dropped to the ground, and ducked around the trees with Prancer all in one lithe movement. Who was shooting at him? And why?

"I want your horse!" a man shouted. "Send him over this way and you can go free!"

Seth snapped his rifle to his shoulder and shot at the voice. The sound boomed out in the silence. Prancer danced back and whinnied in alarm, plowing up the snow around him.

A shot spit up snow and dirt near Seth's feet. He froze. Where was the man?

"You send your horse to me now or I'll shoot you dead on the spot!"

Seth hesitated a moment longer. He couldn't just let someone steal his horse! Suddenly another shot rang out and plowed into the ground at his feet. On the other hand, he couldn't get himself shot over a horse either. What would Diane and Mor do without him?

"You win!" Anger raced through him at the thought of losing Prancer. "I'm sending the horse out! Hold your fire!" Seth pulled off the bedroll he always carried behind the saddle, hooked the reins over the saddle horn, and slapped Prancer's rump. "Go, feller!"

Prancer bobbed his head and walked away from the trees toward the man in hiding.

"Turn your back and don't turn around 'til the count of fifty!" the man shouted.

Seth frowned. The man's voice was familiar, but he couldn't place it. Shrugging impatiently, Seth flung the bedroll over his shoulder and turned his back. He did not wait to the count of fifty, but at the sound of galloping hoofbeats heading away from town, he turned and walked slowly toward town. Anger raged inside him that someone would actually stop him in broad daylight and steal his horse.

His rifle in his left hand and his bedroll draped over his shoulder, Seth strode past the livery where the sheriff's big appaloosa he called App and Bobby's horse, Spade, stood in the corral. He reached the wooden sidewalk and headed for the sheriff's office located between the barber shop and the mortician's office. A wooden SHERIFF'S OFFICE sign swayed and creaked in the cold wind. Across the street a team and wagon stood in front of Jack Cannon's general store, but no one was on the sidewalks on either side of the narrow rutted street. Was Macee at her pa's store or in the jail talking with Bobby?

Seth pushed open the heavy door and stepped inside a small room heated to summer heat by a tiny stove in the corner. Heat stung Seth's face and burned the back of his neck. Roy Prescott sat behind his scarred wooden desk looking through handbills. His gray shirt was open to reveal lighter gray underwear and the brown column of his thick neck. He was a few years older than Seth, medium build and strong as a workhorse. His white stetson, gun and holster hung on a hook on the wall to his left.

"Howdy, Sheriff," Seth said.

He looked up, then smiled, showing crooked teeth and clear hazel eyes. "Seth McGraw. What brings you to my office?"

Seth peeled off his coat before he melted down into his boots. "My horse was stolen!"

Roy Prescott shot to his feet. "You don't say! Morgan Clements was in a couple of days ago and said he had a horse stolen."

"I know he thought one was missing. Did you look for it?"

"Yes, but I couldn't find anything. Not with all this snow." Roy sat back down and motioned for Seth to take the only other chair in the room. It was a straight-back oak chair with a deep scratch across the back. "What does your horse look like?"

"Prancer - a tall bay with a blaze down his face and my brand on his rump."

Roy jotted down the information, then looked up with a smile. "How's your pa?"

"Just fine. The family likes Oregon. They don't have an icy winter or blistering summer to deal with."

"Ever think of joining them?"

Seth shrugged, "At times, but I have my place and I don't want to lose it."

Roy rubbed a thick hand over his short brown hair. "I hear you have a baby son."

Seth tensed, but managed to nod.

"Congratulations! Me and my wife sure want a son. We got two fine girls, but a man needs a son. Don't you think?"

"I reckon so." Seth started to stand.

"Macee Caulder was in earlier. She said you might be in."

Seth flushed and sank back down. "Bobby Ryder."

"I figured you'd want to talk to me about him. Macee Caulder said Bobby Ryder couldn't have killed Goddard."

Seth gripped the brim of his hat and suddenly felt icy cold even though the room was near to a hundred degrees. "Don't you believe her?"

"Sorry to say, I don't. Macee always was one to lie for Bobby Ryder. Why shouldn't she be lying now?"

Seth's stomach knotted painfully. He wanted to lie in the worst way, but he had to tell the truth even if it meant Bobby was set free. "She's right, Roy. Bobby was at my place the past couple of days. He left this morning after Goddard was already dead."

"You don't say! I'll be horn-swoggled!" Roy jerked open the drawer and grabbed up the keys. "I reckon I have to turn that scallywag loose."

"You don't care much for him, do you?"

"I'd as soon spit on him as look at him. He flirted with my wife and turned her head. Almost left me, but Bobby wouldn't marry her."

"How'd you forgive your wife?"

Roy shrugged, "With God's help. That's how."

"Doesn't what happened between them come to you from time to time and make you want to kill Bobby?"

"Sure does, but I put it aside. I put it aside every time. I won't let Bobby ruin my life even one more day. If I spend all my time thinking on him, I figure it's like he's running my life. I won't have that! God is in control of my life. Not Bobby Ryder!"

Suddenly it hit Seth. He'd allowed Bobby to rule *his* life the last ten months! All along he'd been so sure God was in control of his life, but it just wasn't true. He'd let Bobby keep him from loving Diane and Mor as he should. He'd let Bobby keep him from being happy and at peace. No longer! Why hadn't he realized sooner what was happening?

"You say Bobby was at your place?"

"Yes. He got trampled by my bull."

"That's what he said, but I thought an irate husband put him in that shape." Roy jangled the keys and wrinkled his forehead. "I reckon I best let him out. He's been moaning and groaning about getting locked up when he don't deserve to be." Roy chuckled. "Seems to me he deserves a lot worse."

Seth grinned. "Like putting me in there with him to go a few rounds. He's stronger than me on a normal day, but being so banged up, I could take him."

"You sure could." Roy clamped a hand on Seth's shoulder and laughed.

Seth sobered. "I sure want my horse back. It crossed my

mind that Bobby was the horse thief Morgan said to watch out for."

"I gave it some thought too. But I couldn't prove anything and Bobby was close-mouthed about anything that would shine a bad light on him."

"How about if I talk to him before you let him go?"

Roy tossed the keys on his desk and nodded. "You go right on in. That door's unlocked. The cell's locked though."

Seth squared his shoulders and opened the heavy door leading to the cell block. Smells of stale food and body odor smote him as he stopped at Bobby's cell. Bobby lay on a narrow cot with his eyes closed and a blanket over him to keep him warm. The heat from the other room barely warmed the area. "I came to talk with you," Seth said sharply.

Bobby sat up, groaned in pain, and pushed himself up off the cot. He didn't want Seth to do him any more favors, but once again he'd have to accept his help. "Tell the sheriff to get me out of here."

"We're going to have a talk first." Seth leaned against the wall and crossed his arms.

Bobby's heart sank. Seth was going to get even for all the years he'd done him wrong.

"I want to know where Morgan's mare is you stole."

Bobby stared at Seth in shock. He'd never expected that. "I didn't steal Morgan's horse!"

"Then who did? Where is it and how can I get it back?"

Bobby ran a hand over his wrinkled shirt. "If I tell you, will you tell the sheriff I couldn't have killed Julius Goddard?"

Seth shrugged.

"Ord Williams took it to pay his gambling debt to Goddard."

Shock ripped through Seth, but he didn't let it show. "Where'd Goddard put it?"

"In a shed behind his house. Nobody would think to look there. Goddard had a buyer for it, but he didn't get a chance to sell it before he died."

"How do you know that?"

Bobby shrugged. "Ord told me." Bobby gripped the cell bars. The line covered with burrs of thread stood boldly out on his cheek. "Tell the sheriff to let me out right now!"

"Not yet, Bobby. Did Ord plan to steal Red Lightning too?"

Bobby forced back a flush. *He'd* planned to steal Red. "Could be."

"I had my bay stolen out from under me just before I reached town. Would Ord steal my bay?"

Bobby stiffened. "Could be." Ord had needed a horse to get to Seth's place to steal Red, but he'd refused to let him use Spade. Ord didn't have the money to buy or hire a horse. Bobby gripped the bars tighter. "I want out of here!" He would not let Ord make the money off Red when it rightfully belonged to him. His stomach knotted. Red didn't belong to him no matter how he tried to convince himself of that. But selling Red would bring him a lot of money.

Seth started for the door, then looked back over his shoulder. His heart hammered and it was hard to say what he had to say. "Bobby, I forgive you for what you did to Diane and me. For several months it's eaten away inside me, but no longer. With God's help I forgive you. Now I'm going to get on with my life and be happy with *my* wife and *my* baby."

Bobby fell back as if he'd been struck. What kind of a man was Seth McGraw? "I don't need you to forgive me!" Bobby shouted angrily. "Get out of here and leave me alone!"

"The sheriff will be right in to set you free. I told him you were at my house and couldn't have killed Goddard."

Bobby trembled, unable to sort out his feelings. Seth had forgiven him! Nobody was that good! But in his heart he knew God was, and Seth served God. Bobby hung his head. He'd gone to the same church, heard the same sermons, read the same Bible until he'd decided he wanted a different life. In agony he pushed aside the thoughts and turned his back on Seth.

With a cry of victory in his heart, Seth walked away from Bobby into the sheriff's overheated office. "You can set him free, Roy."

"Did you learn anything?"

Seth nodded. "Where Morgan's horse is. Ord took it to pay his gambling debt to Goddard. I'll get it and return it to Morgan."

"Thanks. Stop by the office before you head home so I can see the horse and know for sure it's Morgan's."

"Will do." Seth tugged on his coat and set his hat on his head. "I'll be back." He opened the door just as Macee reached it. She looked chilled to the bone.

"Seth!" she cried in relief. "Thank you for coming!"

Seth nodded. "The sheriff's just ready to set Bobby free."

"Good. I'll be out to your place later to get the rest of my things."

Seth tipped his hat and walked away.

Macee hurried inside, thankful for the warmth. She

dropped her coat over the chair and said, "Sheriff, could I talk to Bobby before you set him free?"

Roy grinned, "I reckon it's a good time to talk straight to him. He can't get away."

Macee nodded, but couldn't manage to smile. She slowly walked back to Bobby, closing the heavy connecting door after her. She didn't want the sheriff to hear the conversation.

"Macee! Good news! The sheriff's letting me go."

"I know. I just saw Seth." Macee took a deep breath and tried to stop her racing heart. "I asked the sheriff to let me talk to you first."

"We can talk somewhere else."

"No!" Macee shook her head hard. "I must tell you in here so you can't get away before you hear me out."

Bobby gripped the bars and scowled in anger. "I hate it in here! Tell the sheriff to unlock the door now!"

Macee shivered, but shook her head. "You're going to listen to me, Bobby. Sit if you want or stand there and glower at me, but I will say what I came to say."

Bobby kicked the bars. "Get it done with. And don't take all day. I think Ord Williams is after Red Lightning. I got to stop him so I can sell Red and get the money."

"That's one of the things I want to say." Macee moistened her dry lips with the tip of her tongue. "I will not help you steal Red like I'd planned. If you do steal Red, I'll tell Seth and the sheriff."

Bobby's face darkened with rage. "Don't you dare!"

Macee backed against the wall. "I don't know how I can love you, Bobby, but I do."

His anger left and he leaned against the bars. Neither did he know how she could love him, truly love him, but she did.

"Get the sheriff to let me out," he said softly.

"I know you love Barney." Macee laced her fingers together.

"Sure, I love the little guy."

"He's your son, Bobby. Your son!"

Bobby fell back a step and shook his head. "No! Don't tell me that! You're saying that to get back at me for doing it to Seth."

Macee shook her head. "Barney is your son. I wanted you to marry me when I first learned I was going to have a baby, but you wouldn't think of such a thing. You wanted to be free. So I married Barney Caulder and I named the baby Barney to try and make up for what I'd done to the dear man I married."

"Why're you telling me this now?"

"To give you another chance. Barney and I both love you. It's not too late for you to love us and for us to become a family."

Dazed, Bobby shook his head. "Are you talking about getting married?"

"Yes! Getting married, being a real family, giving ourselves to the Lord, going to church, having a home of our own."

Bobby shook his head again. "I can't. I won't! How can you say you love me, then try to fence me in that way?"

"Marriage is not being 'fenced in,' Bobby. It's being together with the people you love. Don't you want to see Barney grow to manhood and be somebody? Do you want to miss all his wonderful years?"

Bobby hung his head. "I could see him grow without being married and tied down."

"But you wouldn't be part of his life. I will not tell him

you're his daddy unless you decide to become part of his life."

"Then I'll tell him."

Macee brushed tears off her lashes and touched the tie of her blue bonnet. "Bobby, if you don't want to marry me, I'm going to leave Broken Arrow. I'll go somewhere and find a husband who'll care for me and Barney. I won't stay here and watch you waste your life the way you've been doing. I won't stay and watch you be shot by an angry husband or be kicked by a horse or gored by a bull."

"How can you leave me if you love me?"

"Because of Barney! I want him to be proud of his father. He could never be proud of you."

Bobby sucked in air and turned away from the pain her words brought. He remembered the years he'd been embarrassed by his pa. Is that what he wanted for Barney? Finally Bobby turned back to Macee. "Take Barney and leave. I don't deserve to be part of your lives."

Macee smiled, "You do deserve to be! And we deserve to be part of your life! But you must make the choice - us, or the life you live now." Macee gripped the bars then looked intently at Bobby. "Give up that life and take us!"

Bobby shook his head. "I can't give it up! It's who I am!"

"No!" Macee reached through the bar to touch him. "You can't want drinking and gambling and loose living instead of me and Barney! There's more to you than that or I wouldn't love you. Nor would Barney. You have charm and a quick wit and a kind heart if you care to show it."

"I'm a worthless cowboy, Macee."

"You can work on Nick Stone's ranch if you want. Pa will let me work in the store. Between both of us we'll make enough money to survive - if we're careful."

"Where would we get the money to send Barney to that higher education you were talking about?"

"We'd figure something out."

"Can't you see, Macee? I don't want to think about things like paying for a house or school or clothes for a kid. It's not my nature to be that way."

"It is, but if you're not interested, then I'll say goodbye now. I'll get my things from Seth's and leave on the Friday stage."

Bobby's heart sank, but he couldn't stop her. It was better for her to leave.

Macee walked slowly toward the door - waiting, hoping Bobby would stop her with a word. He didn't. Tears filled her eyes as she walked into the office, grabbed her coat, and hurried out into the biting wind.

The sheriff jangled the keys and walked slowly back to the cell. "How come the lady was crying so hard?"

Bobby's heart turned over. Did she really love him enough to cry over him? "Let me out of here, Sheriff. I got things to do."

"Like break another heart? Bobby, God loves you. He doesn't like the wrong you do, but he loves you. So does Macee Caulder. Now that's a lot more than some people have. Some people don't have anyone to love them and they don't know God does. They live in misery. Is that what you want?"

"Unlock the door, Sheriff!" Bobby struggled against the ache in his heart. If he ignored it, it would go away and he could go back to living just the way he wanted.

The sheriff swung the door wide. "I put Spade in the livery, so you can pick him up there."

"What's the bill?"

"I already took care of it."

Bobby jerked on his jacket, picked up his gun and clamped his hat on his head. He rushed outdoors into the biting wind. With his head down and his shoulders bent, he half-ran, half-walked to the livery to get Spade.

At the sound of a buggy stopping outside the house, Diane ran to the window. Had Kate returned? Diane pulled aside the curtain and looked out. It was the peddler, Isaac Washington! He came every other month with his wares. Snow whirled across the ground under his red and blue wagon and around the big hooves of his team of work horses. Their tails and forelocks were braided with ribbons of red and blue intertwined in the braids. They looked very festive on such a dreary day.

Diane grabbed her coat and bonnet and rushed out to meet the peddler. He jumped down from the seat, pulled off his wide-brimmed white hat and bowed so low his curly head almost brushed the ground. His teeth gleamed white in his black face.

"Good afternoon, Isaac!" she cried excitedly.

"Afternoon, Mrs. McGraw. I brought you something real special today."

Her eyes sparkled, "You did? What?"

"Come around to the back and I'll show you." Isaac unlatched the back doors and flung them wide. A medium sized black dog with short hair and pointed ears jumped up and gave a happy bark. "It's Jack! I got him from a family moving back east that didn't want to be bothered with him."

Diane held her hand out and Jack sniffed it.

"I thought about you and Seth without a dog on the place. Jack here can herd cattle and sheep. And he's a good watch dog."

"I'll take him! Thank you, Isaac!" Diane hugged Jack and he licked her cheek.

"Tie him up a couple of days until he knows this is his home, then you won't have any problem with him running off." Isaac snapped a rope on Jack's collar and motioned for him to jump down to the ground. Jack leaped down and stood beside Isaac.

"Seth will be happy when he sees Jack." Diane looped the rope around a porch spindle. "I'll take him to the barn later. Now, what do you have for me today?"

"How about a fancy valentine for the man of your dreams?" Isaac held up a red and white valentine card decorated with flowers and cupid shooting an arrow.

"It's early for that, isn't it?"

"It's already February, Mrs. McGraw."

Diane gasped. She'd lost track of time. "Then I'll buy a valentine today." It would be fun to see Seth's face when she gave him one.

"And a big box of chocolates?" Isaac held up a box of candy decorated with a red bow and white paper roses.

Diane hesitated, then she remembered that Seth liked chocolate candy. "I'll take a box. But now show me the wares I should buy. I need thread and a pack of needles. And a pair of levis for Seth. A bolt of flannel, too."

Soon she had all she needed. "I'll get your money. Come inside for a cup of hot coffee and some bread and jam." She knew that was his favorite thing to eat in the middle of the afternoon. If he stopped in the evening he'd eat supper with them. Then he liked roast beef cooked with potatoes, carrots, and onions. And a yellow cake with whipping cream on top.

Much later Diane hunched down in her coat and walked Jack to the barn. It seemed so quiet with Isaac gone and Mor asleep again.

She opened the barn door and Red nickered. Diane walked Jack to Red's stall. "Jack, meet Red."

Jack jumped up on the stall door and touched noses with Red. Diane laughed, then led Jack to a stall near the front door. "You can sleep in here, Jack." Diane tied him in a stall and gave him a pan of water and some scraps from dinner. "I'll be back before dark to milk the cow and check on you."

Diane braced herself to once again step outside in the icy wind. She was thankful it wasn't snowing or Seth would never get back from town tonight.

She stepped outside and latched the barn door closed, then she stopped short. Prancer stood a few feet away with his reins dangling and his saddle on. Where was Seth? He'd never leave a horse like that in this weather.

She glanced around, but saw only the buildings, the windmill, and the rolling hills covered with snow. She cupped her hands around her mouth and shouted, "Seth? Where are you?"

Ord Williams stepped around the corner of the barn and Diane cried out in sudden fear.

"Don't be scared of me, Diane Clements," Ord said with a toothless smile. His head was covered with a wooly cap that covered his ears. His face was red with the wind and he badly needed a shave. One pantleg was ripped revealing red longjohns underneath.

Diane relaxed slightly. She'd never known Ord to be dangerous. "Where's Seth?"

"Still in town. He sent me out to get Red Lightning for him."

Fear trickled down Diane's spine. Seth would never send Ord Williams after anything - especially not an expensive horse like Red Lightning. "Let's take Prancer in the barn out of the wind and talk about it."

Ord shivered and nodded.

Diane led Prancer inside. He nickered and Red answered. Jack strained at his rope and barked. "Quiet, Jack!" Diane left Prancer standing and patted Jack until he settled back down.

Ord huddled into himself and looked older than his fifty years. "I could do with a drink. You got anything?"

"Coffee? I made a fresh pot a while ago and you're welcome to it."

Ord scowled, "I need something stronger. But you and Seth don't hold to strong drink, do you?"

"No, we don't. You'll have to wait until you get back to town for that."

Ord trembled and rubbed his gloved hand across his mouth. "I need a drink something fierce."

"I'm surprised you came way out here without bringing a bottle with you."

"I didn't have no money. Seth said he'd pay me if I'd get the big red horse for him." Ord swayed and almost fell. "I didn't reckon for it to take so long or to be so cold."

Diane tipped a bucket upside down. "Sit down and rest a bit."

"Think I will." Ord sank to the bucket and hunched into himself. "Can't get warm."

"I have a hot fire going in the house. And a comfortable rocking chair." She had to keep him there until Seth returned. But how could Seth get home with Prancer here? Had something dreadful happened to Seth? Diane forced back a shiver.

"I got to get back to town." But Ord didn't make a move.

"Coffee with plenty of sugar and cream. I could make you a bite to eat. Are you hungry?"

"No. Thirsty. Mighty thirsty. And cold!" Ord shivered so hard he almost fell off the bucket.

"Come inside and sit by the stove in the rocking chair. You can relax, get warm, then go back to town."

"Maybe I should."

"I'll put Prancer in a stall until then." Diane led Prancer to a stall and shut the door. She was afraid to unsaddle him in case Ord got suspicious. She had to do something to keep him here until Seth got home.

What if he didn't come home?

Her heart froze at the terrible thought and she couldn't move.

How could she survive without him?

CHAPTER 10

Diane took a deep, steadying breath, silently asked God to protect Seth, then walked to where Ord Williams sat on the bucket. Jack whined and Red bumped against her stall. Diane took Ord's arm and lifted him. "Come inside with me to get something to eat and to warm yourself."

Suddenly Ord reared back and his eyes looked wild. "Don't you touch me! I came to get Red Lightning and that's just what I'll do! I won't let that Bobby Ryder beat me to that big, red horse and all that money!"

Diane's heart stood still. Was Ord saying Bobby was planning to steal Red? That would sure answer some of her questions about why Bobby had been here on Worth's birthday and why he'd hidden Spade in the pasture. The bull had stopped Bobby from carrying out his terrible plan. "Come to the house and get warm first, Ord."

"No. No, no, no, no! I'm taking Red right now!" Ord lurched down the aisle toward Red Lightning.

Diane hesitated, then ran after Ord and caught his arm. He was taller and broader than she was, but in a weakened condition or he would have been able to toss her aside like a feather. "Stop, Ord! You need to go inside with me and get warm and eat something or you'll fall out of the saddle on your way to town. Do you want to freeze to death in the snow?"

He crumpled to the floor and moaned in pain as he held his middle. "I need a drink. Get me a drink!"

"Then come inside with me!" She had to get back in the house to fix the fires and check on Mor. As cold as it was it wouldn't take long for the house to cool right down if the fires did go out. She tugged on his arm and finally he struggled to his feet. She walked him out of the barn, latched the door, and walked slowly across the yard. He leaned heavier and heavier on her until she thought her knees would buckle. Wind whistled around the house and blew loose snow in a whirlwind across the yard. The windmill squawked, but couldn't twirl because it was locked down.

Finally Diane stepped inside the kitchen, thankful for the warmth. She eased Ord down on a chair and helped him take off his coat and hat. His thin, gray hair stood on end and his shirt was wrinkled and dirty and smelled of beer.

Diane hurried to the stove and filled a mug with hot, black coffee. She set it in front of Ord and said, "Drink it!"

He lifted it to his lips and drank, then grimaced.

Diane fixed the fire, then ran to the bedroom to check on Mor. Thankfully he was sleeping soundly. She stopped in the front room to shake down the ashes and fix the fire, then rushed back to the kitchen. Ord was gone and the door was wide open, letting in a blast of icy air. Ord's coat and hat still hung on the peg. "That man!"

Diane slipped on her coat and bonnet, caught up Ord's coat and hat and ran outdoors. She stumbled over him sprawled on the porch steps and almost fell headlong. She bent down to him, but couldn't tell if he was out cold or asleep - or worse yet, dead. Silently she prayed for him.

How was she ever going to get him inside? If she didn't, he'd freeze to death.

She bent over him again and slapped his cheeks. "Ord! Wake up! Come inside!" She waited, but he didn't respond. She held her face down close to his to see if he was still breathing. She felt his breath against her face and she sighed in relief, "At least he's alive."

She slapped his face again, but he didn't stir. How was she going to get him inside? He was too heavy for her to carry alone. Suddenly she remembered how she and Worth (when they were children) had moved a dead cow from the doorway of the barn into the yard without help. They had used a lever and a rope and the side of the shed to prop the lever against. That's how she'd move Ord!

Diane spread Ord's coat over him and tugged his cap down over his ears, then ran inside for Seth's rope coiled on a peg in the back room. She ran out the back door for the pole she used to prop up the middle of the sagging clothes-line and carried it to the kitchen door to use as a lever. Tying the loop around Ord's chest and under his arms with the knot at his back, she pulled the rope taut and tied it around the middle of the pole. She took a deep breath, made sure the end of the pole was braced against the door frame, then pulled the free end of the pole toward her, inching Ord along the porch toward the doorway. The rope slipped to the bottom of the pole against the door frame. She pulled it taut and tied it again, then repeatedly pulled on the pole, inching Ord along. After a time her arms ached and she wanted to give up, but she pulled the rope taut, retied it and once more used the pole as a lever. Finally Ord lay in the doorway. She ran to the door leading to the back room and used the frame to prop the pole against, and again inched Ord forward until finally he lay far enough inside that she could shut the door to block out the icy wind. The kitchen was cold but she'd worked up a sweat.

She hung up her coat and covered Ord with his coat that had fallen off earlier. She sank to a chair and breathed deeply. Finally she had the strength to fix the fire. From the bedroom she got a pillow and blanket for Ord, hung up his coat and hat, then sat down again. Ord's breathing was shallow, but he was breathing. At times he moaned and jerked his legs and arms. Mor cried and she carried him back to the kitchen to feed him so she could keep an eye on Ord. She didn't want him running back outdoors once her back was turned. She could also watch out the window for Seth.

After she finished feeding and burping Mor, she held him in her arms, smiled at him and talked to him. His mouth moved and she gasped, "He smiled! I know he smiled! Wait'll I tell Seth!"

Her heart sank. Seth wouldn't care if Mor smiled or not. She pulled Mor close and held him a long time. Later she heard hoofbeats and looked out the window. It was Seth on Pa's sorrel mare!

Diane carried Mor to his cradle, then ran back to the kitchen, tugged on her coat, tied her bonnet in place, and ran outside while she pulled on her mittens. Seth was just opening the barn door.

"Seth!"

The wind carried her shout away and he didn't hear. She raced across the yard and stepped into the barn just as Jack growled and lunged at Seth.

Seth pulled up his rifle but, before he could fire, Diane

shouted, "Don't Seth!" She turned to the dog, "Jack! Down!"

Jack sank to the floor and whined.

Seth lowered the rifle and turned to Diane with his brows cocked. "Where in the world did that dog come from?"

Diane smiled shakily. She wanted to fling her arms around Seth and hold him fiercely. "From the peddler. Come and meet him."

"Do I want to?"

Diane took Seth's gloved hand and led him to Jack. "Hold your hand out to him."

"Do I dare?" Seth asked with a laugh. It was hard to concentrate on the dog with Diane so close to him. He held out his hand and Jack sniffed him, then wagged his tail.

"His name is Jack and he belongs to us now. He's a very good dog. He can herd cattle and sheep and is a good watchdog."

Seth laughed, "He sure is a watchdog! If he'd been loose in here, I might be dead on the floor."

"No!" Diane caught Seth's arm, "Don't even say it!"

Seth smiled at her and his heart jumped wildly, then he glanced up at a movement in the nearby stall. He stepped toward the stall with a frown. "Prancer! How'd he get here?"

Diane told him the story as quickly as she could. "I must get back inside before Ord does something to hurt himself or Mor."

Seth locked Morgan's sorrel in a stall and ran back to the house with Diane. Ord still lay on the floor. Seth tried to wake him as Diane went to check Mor.

"How come you rode Pa's horse home?" Diane asked as

she hung up their coats and sat at the table.

Seth gave up trying to wake Ord, sat beside Diane, and told her what had happened.

"How awful!" She squeezed his hand. "I'm glad you're all right."

"Me too." He wouldn't want anything to keep him from Diane.

She bit her lip, "How about Bobby?"

Seth tensed, then pushed the tension away. Bobby no longer ruled his life! Seth told about his meeting with Bobby. "When I stopped to see the sheriff after I picked up your pa's horse, Bobby was gone. Roy said Macee talked to Bobby and left crying. I reckon she found out what a no-good he is."

"She probably did. He sure had me fooled for a long time."

Seth sat very still. "Do you know the truth now?"

"Yes." She hung her head. "I want to tell you something, Seth, but I know it'll hurt you."

He caught her hand. "Don't say it. It doesn't matter." He was sure she was going to tell him Mor was Bobby's. "Bobby can't hurt us any longer."

Tears sparkled in her eyes. "You knew about...about, you know...Bobby...." She couldn't admit her love for Bobby aloud. "Yet you still married me?"

"Yes." His eyes softened. "I couldn't help myself."

"Why?" she whispered. She had to hear the words from his lips.

Before Seth could speak, Ord sat bolt upright and flung back the blanket. "Bobby can't have Red! I get him and the money he'll bring!"

Seth and Diane stared at Ord in surprise. Seth lifted Ord

onto a chair with his arms folded on the table propping him up.

"Ord, it's me, Seth McGraw. Is Bobby going to steal Red Lightning?"

Ord blinked and rubbed an unsteady hand across his grizzled face. "What am I doing in here?"

"You came to get Red Lightning," Diane said softly. "But you fell down outdoors and I brought you in."

Ord moved restlessly. "I wanted to use Spade to ride out here, but Bobby wouldn't let me. He was in jail and he couldn't ride Spade, but he still wouldn't let me." Ord grinned. "I got a horse anyway and I rode out here to get Red."

Seth clamped a hand on Ord's shoulder. "You can go to jail for stealing a horse, you know."

"I had to pay Goddard or he was going to take my wife and sell her to a brothel in Kansas."

Seth and Diane exchanged startled looks.

Ord shuddered. "I couldn't let him take Janice." He pushed himself up. "I got to get back to make sure Goddard don't take her."

"Goddard's dead, Ord," Seth said gently. "He won't bother Janice or anyone else."

"Dead? You sure about that? I saw him last night and he was yelling at me for not paying him. I even gave him Morgan's sorrel mare but he said I must've forgot, 'cause he didn't have it."

"He did have the mare locked in his shed, but I got her back."

"You say Goddard's dead?"

Seth nodded as he fixed the fire. "I'll get you back to town, Ord. Your wife is probably worried about you."

Diane glanced outdoors and shivered. "It's so late, Seth!"

"You're right." Seth peered out the window. Daylight was fading fast. He turned to Ord. "You can sleep here tonight, then tomorrow morning after chores, I'll take you home."

Ord groaned and held his stomach. "I need a drink bad. You got a drink?"

"No, but Diane will feed you supper and give you buttermilk to drink. Buttermilk will help your stomach." Seth pulled on his coat and picked up the milk pail. "I'm going to milk the cow and get the eggs. Want to go with me, Ord?"

"I reckon so. If I can walk." Ord pushed himself up and awkwardly pulled on his cap and coat. "You sure Goddard's dead?"

"I'm sure. The sheriff thought Bobby killed him, but he didn't."

"Who did?"

Seth looked intently at Ord, "Did you?"

"No!" Ord groaned, "Maybe I did when I was drunk and forgot."

Seth shook his head. "You think on it and see if you can remember." Seth opened the door, glanced at Diane and smiled, then walked out with Ord.

Diane hurried to the window and watched Seth walk slowly across the yard with Ord beside him. "Seth's a nice man," Diane whispered. But she'd always known that. He turned and looked back at the house, saw her, and lifted his hand to her. She waved back, her heart bursting with love. She gasped and clamped her hand over her mouth. She loved him! She loved him with her whole heart! She loved him passionately like Ma loved Pa!

Diane walked to a chair and sank down weakly before her legs gave way. Her heart was beating loud enough to wake Mor. "I love Seth!" she whispered, then said it aloud.

She laughed and twirled about the room. "I love him!" When had loved blossomed in her heart? Had it been there all along, but hidden from her because of her obsession with Bobby?

She ran to the window just in case she could get another glimpse of Seth. He was not in sight and she sighed heavily. Would she have the courage to tell him she loved him?

She lifted her chin, "I'll tell him even if I don't have the courage!"

Just then Macee drove up in a buggy. She parked close to the porch and jumped to the ground. Even in her warm coat and bonnet she looked cold. She looked almost wild, Diane thought.

Diane flung the door wide. "Macee, I thought you weren't coming back today. Is something wrong?"

Macee ran to Diane and gripped her arms. "Bobby is planning to steal Red. I came to stop him. I won't let him continue to hurt you and Seth! Not after all you've done for us!"

Diane grabbed her coat. "Let's go tell Seth. He's in the barn."

They hurried down the porch steps. Her face set, Macee lifted a shotgun from her buggy.

"What are you going to do with that?" Diane asked in alarm.

"Stop Bobby!"

Diane darted a look around. It was still light enough to see. "I don't think he's here."

"I do! He was determined to sell Red and the buyer's in town right now waiting. I saw him and that's why I came here." Macee walked with determined steps across the snowy yard.

Diane ran to keep up with her. She opened the barn door and let Macee walk in first. They both stopped short. Bobby held Seth and Ord at gunpoint. Red was standing in the aisle of the barn. Bobby held Red's halter with one hand, and his .44 with the other.

Diane ran to Seth and slipped her hand through his arm.

He didn't take his eye off Bobby, but he clasped his hand over Diane's.

"Get out of here, Macee," Bobby said grimly.

Macee lifted the shotgun to her shoulder. "Drop the gun, Bobby," she said in a dead, calm voice.

Bobby stared at her in shock, "You won't shoot me."

"I will if I have to. I won't let you steal Red. Put her back in the stall and come with me right now!"

"You listen to her, Bobby," Seth said softly. "You don't want to swing from the end of a rope just for a little cash in your hand."

Diane trembled.

Ord shook his finger at Bobby. "I bet my bottom dollar you killed Goddard."

Bobby angrily shook his head, "I did not!"

"Janice Williams did," Macee said.

Diane gasped and Seth whistled in surprise.

Ord jerked around with a shocked look on his face and stared at Macee. "My wife killed Goddard? That woman's too religious to kill anyone. Or I'd be dead by now."

"Janice confessed to the sheriff." Macee looked only at Bobby, but she was talking to the others too. Jack whined and tugged against his rope. "She said Goddard abducted her and was planning to sell her to a brothel in Kansas. She grabbed for his gun, they struggled, and she shot Goddard. She was afraid to step forward until late this afternoon."

"I'll be," Ord said, shaking his head. "I'll be."

"She won't have to go to jail since it's self-defense," Seth said.

"That wife of mine!" Ord said and shook his head again. "There's a whole lot more to her than I thought."

"You should learn to appreciate her," Diane said sharply.

Macee stepped closer to Bobby. "Put the gun away, Bobby, and leave with me."

Bobby shook his head. "You love me, Macee. You won't shoot me."

"I love you and I will do what it takes to make you leave here with me without Red Lightning."

"Do as she says, Bobby," Seth said again. "In your heart you want to do the right thing. You were always that way, but too many times you wouldn't listen to your heart."

"What do *you* know, McGraw?" Bobby waved the .44. "You don't even know I lied to you about Diane."

Diane frowned at Bobby. She felt Seth's tension. What had Bobby told Seth?

"Every story I told you was a lie. You lived in agony because of a lie!"

With a cry of rage Seth lunged at Bobby and wrestled the gun from his hand, dropped it to the floor, then caught Bobby by the throat in a strangle-hold.

Diane cried out in fear, then quickly caught Red and led her back to her stall before she got frightened. Diane watched Seth scuffling with Bobby. What lies had Bobby told Seth?

"You lied to me and I believed you! What a fool I was!" Seth pulled back his fist to smash Bobby in the face, then dropped his hand to his side. "No! I won't do it!"

"What's the matter, McGraw? Can't you stand the thought of seeing my blood on your hand or your barn floor?" Bobby sneered.

Seth squared his shoulders. "I already forgave you, Bobby. I don't need to hit you or get even." Seth pushed Bobby toward Macee. "Go with Macee. If you have any sense left, you'll marry her and make her and your son happy."

Diane ran to Seth and slipped her hands through his arm again. She clung to him as if she'd never let him go.

He covered her hands with his and smiled into her wide eyes. She had not been with Bobby! Bobby was not Mor's father! Seth's pulse leaped. That precious baby belonged to him! His own flesh and blood!

Ord caught Bobby's arm and grinned at him. "You and me could ride back to town together and get roaring drunk."

Bobby looked at Ord and his wasted life. Suddenly Bobby knew he didn't want to waste his life a minute longer. Why had it taken so long to realize that? He put aside his pride and walked to Macee. He looked deeply into her eyes. "Go ahead and shoot me if you want to. I deserve it."

Her lips trembled. "No, you don't. You deserve to be loved just like the rest of us." Macee stood the shotgun down against the nearest stall and held her hand out to Bobby.

He caught her hand and held it against his heart. "I'm ready to get married and make all the changes you talked about. If you still want me."

"I do. We'll get married tomorrow." Macee smiled into

Bobby's eyes, then turned to Seth and Diane. "You're invited to the wedding. At the church at eleven in the morning."

"We'll be there," Seth said.

Diane nodded in agreement.

Macee loaded the rest of her things in the buggy. Bobby helped Ord into the back seat and tied Spade to the back of the buggy. Then Bobby drove away with Macee snuggled tight against his side, looking happy and at peace.

Standing in the yard, Diane hugged Seth's arm. "I like happy endings."

"So do I." He smiled at her, then pulled away. "I have to get the chores done and you have to check on Mor and make supper."

"I reckon you're right." Diane wrinkled her nose at him, then ran to the house. She'd make Seth the best supper he'd had in a long time!

Tying on her apron, she felt the paper in her pocket. She pulled it out and ran her finger over the heart with her name in it. Laughing, she found a pencil, drew another heart and wrote "Seth" inside it. She laid the paper at Seth's place at the table so he'd be sure to see it.

Diane lit the lamps and fixed the fire again, then peeled potatoes. She put them on to boil, poured a jar of green beans into a pan, mixed up a batch of biscuits and pushed them into the oven to bake. Opening a jar of canned beef, she unrolled the slices and laid them in a heavy cast iron skillet on the hottest part of the stove. Soon the kitchen was full of mouth-watering aromas.

Seth opened the door and sniffed deeply. "Smells like home," he said happily. The wind caught the paper and blew it to the floor under the table. Seth set the milk and eggs down, pulled off his coat, then bent to pick up the paper. "What's this?"

Diane waited, her breath caught in her throat.

Seth saw the heart he'd drawn, then the one Diane had drawn. He looked at her intently and pushed the paper in his pocket as he slowly walked to her. He stood close to her without touching her, noticing the way a blonde curl clung to her flushed cheek, the way her lips trembled slightly as she waited for him to speak, the way her eyes turned bluer as he looked at them. "My heart is full and overflowing with you," he said tenderly.

A weakness swept over her and, for a minute, she couldn't speak. She liked the flame of his hair, the way his freckles spread across his nose, the passion of his lips, the firm set of his chin. "You are the husband of my dreams," she whispered. "The only husband I'll ever desire."

He lowered his head and brushed his lips across hers, then stepped back quickly. "I'd better take care of the milk and eggs before I forget about them." Taking care of the milk and eggs was the farthest thing from his mind.

Diane flushed and nodded. "I'll put supper on before it burns." Putting supper on was the farthest thing from her mind.

Seth put the milk and eggs in the back room to cool, then washed his face and hands. Before he could sit at the table, Mor cried.

Diane set the pan of biscuits on a trivet. "I'll get him."

"No!" Seth's arms ached to hold his son. "Let me."

Diane stopped in stunned silence. She watched Seth walk away, then hurried after him. A miracle had happened! Silently Diane thanked God for it.

In the bedroom Seth bent over the cradle and gently

lifted Mor in his arms. This was his son! His and Diane's! "You are a precious baby, Morgan Clements McGraw."

Diane stepped quietly to Seth's side. She was almost afraid to say anything and ruin the blessed moment. "He has your mouth."

"Do you think so?" Seth studied Mor's mouth and finally nodded. "He does! And your pa's hair and eyes." Tears stung Seth's eyes. How much he'd missed by believing Bobby's lies!

Diane leaned her head against Seth's arm and looked down at their baby. "I want the next one to have red hair."

"Or blonde like yours."

Diane closed her eyes as joy leaped inside her. Whatever had been bothering Seth was finally gone! Thank God!

Mor squirmed and cried.

"I guess you'd better feed him." Reluctantly Seth held him out to Diane.

"We'll go to the kitchen and eat our supper while he's nursing."

"A family dinner," Seth said with a laugh as he slipped his arm around Diane's shoulder.

His touch sent a wave of love crashing over her and it was hard to concentrate on what she was doing.

Later Diane gave Seth his first lesson in changing a diaper. "You'll learn not to stick him with a pin," Diane said with a giggle.

"I don't know about that." Seth looked at his big hands. "But I'll try."

Seth rocked Mor until he fell asleep, then unwillingly laid him in his cradle and watched him. "He's the most beautiful baby in the world."

"I agree! Maureen said he was only in our small part of

the world."

"She would say that," Seth chuckled. "I saw Maureen today. She was excited because she got to write the story about Goddard's death."

"Did you see Alane?"

"Not today. Why?"

Diane told Seth about the letter Alane had written. "I told her not to send it. I didn't want her to marry a man without loving him. I said love couldn't happen." Diane smiled and wondered if she should continue. She knew she had to in order to break down every barrier between her and Seth. "I was wrong. A woman can fall in love with her own husband and that love can grow until it consumes her."

His pulse leaping, Seth turned away from the cradle and gave Diane his full attention. "A husband can fall deeper in love with his wife even when he's loved her since he was a boy."

"That long?" Diane asked in awe.

Seth took Diane's hands in his. "Your pa still kisses your ma at every opportunity he can find. Will you want my kisses years from now?"

Diane nodded. "I'm starved for your kisses, for your love."

Her words filled him with happiness. She wanted him, not Bobby Ryder!

Diane pulled her hands free and slid them around Seth's neck. "I love you, my darling, magnificent husband."

With a glad cry Seth pulled her close and buried his face in her hair. "I love you! I loved you when you were a little girl in pigtails and I love you right this minute and I'll love you when your hair is gray!"

Her heart burst into flame and she turned her face to find

his lips. "Kiss me. Kiss me the way you did in the snow on Worth's birthday."

Seth covered her mouth with his and kissed her with all the built-up passion and hunger that he'd kept locked inside. No longer did he have to restrain himself! She was his wife and he loved her!

Diane returned his kisses with matching passion and hunger that she'd never known she could feel for Seth McGraw, the husband God had chosen for her!